A Branch Too Weak

Richard Roux

GREENHORN MOUNTAIN BOOKS

Greenhorn Mountain Books

Published by Greenhorn Mountain Books

Bakersfield, CA

greenhornmountainbooks@gmail.com

ISBN-13: 978-0-692-93811-9

Full Page Map: Ensigns & Thayer, Map of the Gold Regions of California, Showing the Routes via Chagres and Panama, Cape Horn, &c., 1849. David Rumsey Map Collection, David Rumsey Map Center, Stanford Libraries.

Contents

Also By Richard Roux

NON-FICTION

Bootleggers, Booze, and Busts: Prohibition in Kern
County, 1919-1933
Bootlegger Tales: More Drips, Drops, and Drams

THE GOLDEN EMPIRE SERIES

A Branch Too Weak
A Good Stock
Love & Loss on the Razor's Edge

OTHER WORKS

The Cave of Treasure (With Jeff R. Smith)

Dedication

———◆———

To the dreamers and doers, those who reach for their goals and push through adversity.

And for my Uncle John Cody, who instilled within me a love for the West when I was a boy.

Mark Twain Quote

———◆———

It was a splendid population—for all the slow, sleepy, sluggish-brained sloths stayed at home—you never find that sort of people among pioneers—you cannot build pioneers out of that sort of material.

It was that population that gave to California a name for getting up astounding enterprises and rushing them through with a magnificent dash and daring and a recklessness of cost or consequences, which she bears unto this day—and when she projects a new surprise the grave world smiles as usual and says, "Well, that is California all over."

Mark Twain, *Roughing It*

Acknowledgments

"History is a guide to navigation in perilous times. History is who we are and why we are the way we are." I tend to take this quote by David McCullough to heart when I think about my books. There are many historians and works on history I have read over the years that continue to have a profound impact on how I view the history of the United States, the history of the American West, and the diverse people who collectively made our nation. To those historians, I have a great deal of respect, and I owe them gratitude.

I'd like to thank and acknowledge the following people, in no particular order, who inspired me to become more connected with the process of accessing history and examining events in new ways. Some, I know, others, I only know through their work. Thank you to Jerry Stanley and Douglas Dodd. Their passion for history and leadership in classes and seminars taught me new perspectives. J.S. Holliday, author of *The World Rushed In*, is an authority on the California Gold Rush. His work helped me better understand this historical event. Bob Powers, author of numerous books, including *Kern River Country*, and Professor William Harland Boyd, author of *A California Middle Ground: The Kern River Country, 1772-1880*, both aided with background information and place names. There is a group of historians who are leaders in what is categorized as the fields of Environmental History and New Western History. Their works helped me shape a new perspective on the history of the West: Richard White (*"It's Your Misfortune and None of My Own": A New History of the American West*); Patricia Nelson Limerick (*The Legacy of Conquest: The Unbroken Past of the American West*); Susan Lee Johnson (*Roaring Camp: The Social World of the California Gold Rush*); and Elliott West (*Growing Up with the Country: Childhood on the Far Western Frontier*).

Lastly, and most of all, I'd like to thank my family, especially my wife and daughter. Their understanding and patience with me have made it possible for this book to be written.

MAP OF THE GOLD REGIONS OF CALIFORNIA.

Showing the Routes via Chagres and Panama, Cape Horn, &c.

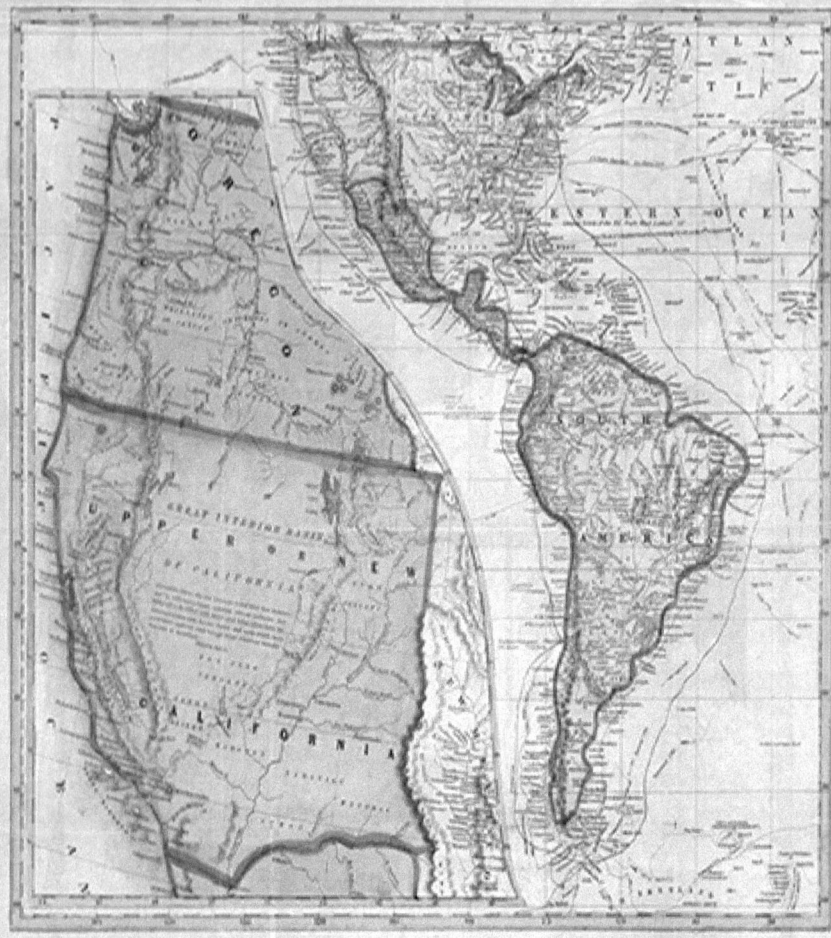

IMPORTANT DIRECTIONS

TO PERSONS EMIGRATING TO
CALIFORNIA.

ROUTE via CHAGRES and PANAMA.

ROUTE BY CAPE HORN.

ANOTHER ROUTE.

DESCRIPTION OF CALIFORNIA,

OR THE NEW
GOLD REGION.

Chapter 1
The Oak

———◆———

To say that it was ancient was an understatement. The towering oak tree possessed all of the markings of an elder in the forest. A grayish, thick bark with deep crags, as if made from shattered glass, ran from its base up to where branches spread out like arms grasping for the sky. The wind gently rustling through the broad multicolored leaves told the ebb and flow of all that the tree had witnessed throughout its long history—a history that was perhaps as old as two hundred years at that point in time. From the husk of an acorn buried in the ground, this majestic tree began as a tiny sprout. Pushing up through rich soil comprised of decaying plant matter and decomposed granite, that delicate sprout began a journey toward the sun; yearning for light, water, and air. Struggling for existence. Striving to play its role in the age-old tale of life and death.

And what an account of history the giant could tell if it were able to talk. Positioned on a ridge 5,000 feet above sea level, the oak was surrounded by others of its kind—black oak, white oak, and scrub oak. There were also pine and fir trees clustered together on the side of hills; giants in their own right, straight and tall. Nearby, gooseberry, cascara, and elderberry bushes dotted the landscape. And grass, lush and green in the spring and the color of straw in the summer and fall, flowed down draws toward meadows of various sizes. Natural water springs sometimes bubbled to the surface, other times they saturated the surrounding ground creating an abundance of thick, green grass and clumps of stinging nettle that swayed in the breeze like flags.

Naturally, the creatures—big and small—that lived in and around the oak tree were part of its life. Birds nested in the cradle of its branches or fed on the insects that traveled daily up and down the tree. Grey squirrels scampered from treetop to treetop, uttering their cacophony of barks and chirp-like sounds to one another. An occasional black bear climbed the tree to feed on acorns or a random bee hive that periodically appeared throughout the years. Deer browsed its tender shoots as it grew in its first decade or so, and then fattened up on the crop of falling acorns season after season. Even a mountain lion or two had either napped in the tree or eaten part of a newly killed deer under its eave-like branches. A shelter, a source of food, a place of rest—that oak tree was many things while only trying to be one.

Not one hundred feet away from its base were a series of large granite rocks. More accurately, they were boulders, relatively flat on the top and low to the ground. Smooth holes, varying in width and depth, were embedded into the top surface of each cluster of rocks, the product of generations of pestles grinding acorns into a grainy substance. These rocks anchored a seasonal encampment of Yokut Indians, maybe even an occasional group of Tubatulabal Indians. For a large portion of the year, family units camped at these and thousands of similar sites to subsist. Men hunted using bows and arrows tipped with obsidian points. Women cared for the young, gathered berries and acorns, and prepared food. Those acorns were pounded and ground until they resembled flour, bitter and inedible until the tannins were leeched by filtering water through the material. The processed acorn mash could then be eaten like a porridge or a pancake, products of human experimentation and ingenuity. The laughter of children, the comfort of conversation, and the singing of songs echoed the rhythm of a people—a people of the mountains, foothills, and valleys. That giant oak and its innumerable kin sustained the lives of those native to the land.

Now, the oak witnessed a new migration of people into what is called the Greenhorn Mountains. The majority of these migrants were eager to seek fortunes in the form of golden flakes, powder, or even nuggets. Gold, with its luster, motivated men to sacrifice, to gamble, to steal, and to kill. It represented the wealth of nations and people. And often, it symbolizes the unity of two people in marriage.

When James Marshall discovered gold on the American River near Coloma in 1848, the lust for gold caused a rush of Argonauts into the Sierra foothills, ballooning the population of a distant California by the end of 1849. The repetitive announcement of strike after strike kicked off the race to gold over and over. And so was the case in 1853 when gold was discovered on Greenhorn Creek near the Kern River. This motivated people to run to the hills...again. One of the routes to known gold-bearing earth in the region was called the Greenhorn Trail. Not suitable for comfortable travel, it was more of a track that ran from Linn's Valley, through Poso Flat, traversed up the side of a mountain to the ridgeline, and then bumped and bucked before dropping off the mountain to the mining claims along Greenhorn Creek and Keyesville. Not more than fifty yards was the distance from that specific oak to the Greenhorn Trail. The number of people passing by the tree had grown steadily as the months and years ticked by; foreigners at the very least, barbarians at their worst.

Each year since its birth, cycles of growth added to what would eventually be the mass of this tree. In fact, a detailed accounting of its growth could be seen if the trunk was laid open and the rings observed. Every ring was a clue to that year. During wet years, the growth rings were wide. And the dry years, so typical of California, were represented by rings spaced close together. The spaces between the rings were not consistent, but what remained true was the size of this oak tree.

Besides the sunshine necessary for the growth of a tree, water is essential. Through a little miracle of nature, leaves use sunlight to convert water and carbon dioxide into the energy necessary to grow. Rain...sweet rain...is feast or famine in the Greenhorn Mountains, as is snow. Less than ten miles away from the oak tree was the wild Kern River, too far away to be a source of water for the tree in question. As was the Poso Creek, at least five miles away. That left the intricate weave of roots that dwelled wide and deep into the ground to provide the water needed for survival. As the saying goes, only the strong survive. A quick look around the forest bolstered this claim, with the stunted trees and sad, brown sticks that dotted the hillsides here and there. Sticks that would have passed for trees if they weren't dead, victims of the competition for water.

But this tree was a survivor. No animal had chewed it to a nub. No storm had blown it over or piled so much snow in its crown that it collapsed under the combined weight. It had escaped lightning and wildfire. And drought, the long-time enemy of California in a physical and human sense, had not claimed it as a victim. Its roots, yearning for water, spider-webbed and radiated down and outward from its base. Every precious vein of water, great or small, was desired and needed. Like an appendage stretched to its limits, the roots were lifelines; connections between the earth and the sky. Life perpetuated. Bark like armor. Rustling leaves in a cool breeze—greens, and browns, and greys. And blood. The year was 1854. At this moment, the liquid seeping into the ground at the base of the tree was blood that belonged to Daniel Vance. Above him, swaying in the gentle breeze as if macabre fruit, was the lifeless body of a man strung up by his neck.

Chapter 2
Gilded Dreams

——————•·•·◆·•·•——————

Nineteen-year-old Daniel Vance, called Danny or Dan by his friends, was a free-spirited young man. Relatively tall at 6 feet, he grew to be a solid 175 pounds; lean muscle coupled with sinewy tendons made him much stronger and agile than he appeared at first glance. But Danny was more than capable of holding his own in most circumstances, whether it be love or war.

He had that wanderlust. As a child on his family's Missouri farm, his early life revolved around the seasons and the toil of everyday chores interrupted only by the periodic times he and other children his age went to school. Up by dawn, Danny collected eggs, milked the cows, cleaned pens, and then ate breakfast. He helped his father in the fields until the early afternoon when he consumed dinner and then focused on more work until the sun went down. There was always something to be done, whether it be chopping wood, clearing lots, plowing fields, tending to or harvesting crops. That monotonous and strenuous work built character, calluses, muscle, and grit. It also made Danny think about having more in life.

Human nature is a peculiar thing. We daydream. Some long for adventure and wealth. Many hope and pray for change, but few people fully realize their aspirations. Instead, they settle into an ever-evolving new normal. That isn't a bad thing. If anything, it pushes the individual and family to fight on. And that was the case for Danny and his family. They were part of the wave of continuous waves expanding westward to reach their version of the American dream. His grandparents emigrated from Ireland to seek a better life. They established shallow roots in Virginia and then Kentucky, each time scraping together enough money from laboring for others to purchase a little scratch of land. All the while, they had children, one of whom was Joseph Vance, the eventual father of Danny.

Joseph, pragmatic and headstrong, grew up in a similar fashion as Danny and his other son, Seth. However, Joseph was a content man. Shortly after marrying his wife Caroline in 1822, Joseph and his bride took what little they owned and moved to Missouri, that relatively new state that had been the focus of much debate and consternation in 1819 and 1820. It was a slave state, per the Compromise of 1820. But, like the majority of people in the South, they were not slave owners. They weren't necessarily against or in favor of slavery, either. Joseph and Caroline were more interested in making a life together—raising a family, growing old together, and just being happy. They intended to make Missouri their forever home. Not all of their children felt the same way. The wild urge to move on and experience new things burned bright in the next generation. Danny's yearning to ramble often flared up like prairie fire.

When the United States went to war with Mexico in 1846, Danny closely followed the news and hoped that he, too, would be able to join that warring adventure. Every update stimulated Danny's imagination and lust for more than life on the farm. In his mind, he was there when Zachary Taylor's forces clashed with the Mexican Army on the Rio Grande. He was there, in spirit, during the Bear Flag Revolt in California with John C. Fremont. And he was proud of his nation, but also melancholy when American forces invaded Mexico City and forced the Mexican government to surrender and accept the terms of the Treaty of Guadalupe Hidalgo in 1848. Danny was eighteen when the war ended. A man, ready to break out on his own. The timing just needed to be right. And so was the case when news from California roared into Missouri.

***

The rider tore up the road faster than was necessary, the big bay kicking up mud and clay as the sure-footed beast raced through the path that was a dry road much of the year.

"Gold...Gold!" the rider's dry voice shouted as he rode into the yard of the Vance's farm. "They found gold," he managed to pant, his warm breath coming out in puffs, like steam from a locomotive.

"What in the world are you talking about Stephen?" Joseph Vance demanded as he stopped the swing of his splitting ax after driving it through a round of oak, making two pieces of wood where there once was one. "Stephen Pryor...have you lost your mind?

"No Mr. Vance...they found gold in California! There's a big rush on now to see the elephant and..."

Joseph interrupted Stephen. "To see the what? Elephant?"

"Oh heck...I heard somebody say that...I guess it means people are heading out to find their fortunes...they want their piece of the action!"

"Fortune," Joseph scoffed. "A bunch of damned fools with gold flakes in their eyes! Why, there's no more of a chance to find your fortune out there as there is here...on the land! At least a man can make something off the land."

About this time Danny came in from a field that he'd been pulling stumps out of, leaving his younger brother, Seth, to take the ox to the small corral to unyoke, feed, and water the animal.

Caught up in the excitement that he was yet to be part of, Danny chimed, "What's this all about? Dad? Stephen?"

Stephen excitedly began, "Danny you won't believe it! There's gold...."

But before he could finish Mr. Vance interrupted, half shouting "Now Stephen...you just hold on a moment. Don't you go filling my son's head with some half-cocked notion about some gold in California!"

"Gold?" Danny asked with cautious interest. "Come on, Pa, let Stephen tell me what he heard. One way or another I'm going to hear about it! Might as well be here and now."

Mr. Vance started to protest further, stopped, thought about ordering Stephen out of his yard, and then just shook his head. "Foolish talk...just plain foolish," he muttered, turning away from the young men, stomped his feet on the boards before the front door, and walked into the house to prepare for supper.

Both Stephen and Danny watched him walk away, little clumps of dirt kicked up with each step. A pall of silence momentarily filled the void. But as soon as Mr. Vance was out of sight, the two boys, barely men, turned to each other, somewhat embarrassed, but fully eager to partake in the gossip.

"You tell me right now what you heard!" Danny demanded of Stephen as he guided him by the arm to some stumps in the shade of an apple tree. They sat down, knees facing each other. Danny was desperately interested and a bit irritated at the patience Stephen had mustered. "Well?"

"Well...I just heard from Mr. Stapleton down at the mercantile that gold was found in California!" Stephen finally blurted out, eyes were wide and gestures overly dramatic as he spoke. "A mountain of gold! It's supposedly the biggest lode ever found!"

Danny cut in, "How much gold? When and where?"

"Just hold on Danny, give me a chance to tell you. Lord Almighty!"

Stephen had Danny's undivided attention. Danny leaned forward, with his elbows on his knees, waiting to hear everything Stephen had to say.

"From what I know, the first strike was at a place called Sutter's Creek last January. Some workers found nuggets in a mill race," Stephen's tone turned serious. "After testing the nuggets, they determined them to be real...genuine gold! Now...they tried to keep it hush-hush, but word spread about their find."

Danny listened, almost trance-like, to this news. Truly, this was unbelievable. Throughout the years, rumors of gold strikes were nothing new. Most of them proved to be false; the others turned out to be inconsequential. With a skeptical ear, Danny continued to take it all in.

"Once others heard about the gold, the race was on! Men ventured up all of these different creeks that feed into what they call the American River. They found gold, too! Danny...gold is being found all over those hills! Men are digging it out of little crevices in the rocks with spoons! With spoons!"

Stephen became more excited as he spoke to Danny. "Even President Polk, two months ago, said that the strike is real! Every day, more and more people are heading to the gold fields...I don't know how many, but I hear it's a sizeable number."

Stephen suddenly stopped his tale. He swallowed hard, took a deep breath, and then squarely looked Danny in the eyes and stated, "And I want some of that gold...I'm going to California and I think you should go with me."

This proclamation did sound as foolish as Danny's father predicted; even irresponsible. To leave home and travel halfway across a continent, with no guarantee of success took more guts and self-confidence than most people had. Comfort, security, routine—that is what most humans gravitate toward and embrace. This was out of the norm for Danny, as well as for Stephen. The family farm offered stability. You probably weren't going to become wealthy working the dirt, but you could make a living. So, leaving home for this kind of endeavor was a gamble emotionally and physically. And that's not even factoring in the monetary cost of such a journey.

Stephen droned on, all the while Danny pondered the opportunity. He did fancy the thought of easy wealth...who wouldn't? But the lingering uncertainties clearly outweighed the enthusiasm he could muster.

Danny shook his head and interrupted stating, "Stephen...I can't...I mean...it just seems too good to be true. We don't know if there is gold there or even if it will still be there by the time we arrive. And how do we get there? I cannot even begin to think how we would start."

Stephen snatched his hat from his head, rubbed his temples in frustration, and slapped his hat against the side of his leg causing a puff of dust to rise from his trousers and hat, quickly drifting away in the cold breeze. He knew, in his heart of hearts, that this was their chance. It was their chance to break free from the monotony of the farm. It was their chance to stand on their own and prove that they were men. It was their chance to succeed...or to fail. Either way, it would be through their efforts alone. But Stephen couldn't do it on his own, or at the very least, he didn't want to do it on his own.

"Please, Danny," Stephen pleaded, "please think about it. We can do this. The hardest part is just getting there."

"For the sake of argument," Danny interjected, "how would we get there?"

"Well if you'd give me a second," an exasperated Stephen huffed, "I'll explain!"

Stephen went on a half-hour harangue—part plea, part educational, but full of vigor—relaying the information he gleaned from Mr. Stapleton and the patrons at his shop.

There were only two feasible routes to the gold fields in California for those living in Missouri; either by ship or overland. They could take a boat down to New Orleans and then take passage on a ship through the Gulf of Mexico and down around the horn and sail up the Pacific Coast to San Francisco. Or they could jump ship in Panama on the Atlantic side, cross over the mountains, and then hope to catch a ship up the rest of the Pacific Coast to California. Once they reached the port of San Francisco, they could then outfit themselves and head to the hills.

The sea route could take as little as four months, or as long as eight months. Depending on decisions made, the distance supposedly ranged from 7,000 to 15,000 miles. And it could be expensive, especially the longer they waited. Rates for passage ranged anywhere between one hundred and one thousand dollars. Stapleton didn't seem to know exactly how much, or if that was in a cabin or the steerage. It didn't matter much, though, because the notion of raising as much as one thousand dollars each, and then purchasing all of the supplies they needed on top of that, was inconceivable. It was depressing for Stephen to even mention the sea route, especially knowing that it did little to convince Danny that the uncertainties were worth the effort.

Perhaps the notion that Stephen was playing the "good news and bad news" game, with the bad news revealed first, was the leverage that he was hoping to use to win

Danny over. The second route, Stephen's Ace in the Hole, was the Overland Trail to the West. They, along with thousands of others could travel this 1,800-mile-long path. West across the Great American Desert, across the Sierra Nevada Mountains, down into the Sacramento River Valley, and up to the American River region. On foot, in a wagon, on a horse or mule, pushing or pulling carts. Depending on conditions, it'd take three to seven months. And the timing would have to be perfect. Leave too soon, and an Argonaut might find swollen rivers and creeks from the snow melt, or they may find that the snow hasn't had time to melt at all. And then there is the threat of heat. Traveling across the desert from the late spring through the early fall is just begging that fireball in the sky to sing down in full force, drying up the earth, the skin, and the will to continue. Of course, if you leave too late, you face complete ruin. All of the natural feed may be gone, you'd still face the brunt of the sun, and then there is the extra, realistic threat of being caught in the mountains during the winter. The plight of the Donner Party of 1846 was no secret. To become snowbound would delay the arrival in California, not to mention hasten an early demise.

From what Stephen could tell, the amount of money needed for the firma terra route was much less. They already had some of the tools they anticipated they would need—picks, shovels, pails—as well as the necessary personal items such as a bedroll, shaving kit, fork, knife, spoon, and tin plate. That would reduce some of the cost of outfitting. But rumors had it that to properly outfit for the trip with 150 pounds of dry goods, cooking gear, several sets of clothes and shoes, materials for washing clothing, a tent, rubber-backed canvas, and tobacco might run as much as two hundred dollars each...maybe even more. But Stephen also heard that the cost could be greatly reduced if they joined a company; a like-minded group of travelers who pooled their money to purchase supplies in bulk, had a leader, voted on decisions, usually had a written set of rules, and members signed a binding contract. It was a sort of home away from home, populated almost exclusively by men of varying ages who completed all the requisite tasks of a household. Cooking, cleaning, mending, and caring for the sick. Companions and confidants, mothers and fathers all rolled into one; strangers and friends, defenders and sometimes rivals.

Stephen painted a rosier picture of traveling across the vast expanse of earth that made up the trans-Mississippi West to the Far West of California. He acted the role of salesman the best that he could.

"Well," Stephen asked, "what do you think...are you with me?"

"I think you've plum lost your mind!" Danny honestly replied, kneading his hat in his hands.

Stephen stammered, "Come on now...there has to be some part of you that is itching to go! What if...just think of the what if! What if this is the only chance we have to leave? Or what if this is the only chance for adventure we have? Or what if we go and we strike it rich?"

"Or what if we find nothing...waste time and money? Or what if we die before we even get there," countered Danny.

With a wry smile, Stephen placed a hand on one of Danny's shoulders, and logically offered, "And what if drought hits the farm? Or plague sweeps through the area? Or we wake up in our bed dead in the morning? Or we die old men with nothing...with nothing ventured and nothing gained."

Since Stephen put it that way, Danny became more comfortable with the conflicting feelings he had inside. He wanted to be a good son, help his father and mother, and be there for his brother. But he was a man. He wanted to chase his dreams; to try his luck in his own way. He wanted to see more of the world. The chance that he was waiting for could be now.

Slowly...steadily...Danny rose to his feet. He paced a few feet, rubbing his chin. Rapid thoughts bounced about that skull of his: He should do it. Can he do it? Would he do it? He will do it!

Reluctantly at first, and then enthusiastically, Danny grabbed Stephen by the hand and arm, firmly confirming their partnership, and joyfully exclaimed "Let's do it! California ho!"

There was much back-slapping and ballyhoo for several minutes before all seriousness set in and the realization that they needed to prepare. They needed money, especially. It was January 1849 and they hoped to jump off for California in April, but surely no later than May. Their decision meant a frantic race to raise the funds, resulting in a string of odd jobs, small loans, and figuring ways to cut costs. Work, beg, borrow, but never steal. Their mammas didn't raise thieves.

They parted, each pledging to keep a tally of the money earned and to meet weekly to discuss their plans to travel to either St. Louis or Independence at a time that seemed way too soon to be probable. Stephen mounted his horse, waved his hat, and rode away.

***

Danny walked to the wash basin located beside the front door to the home that the Vance family built for themselves. The family home. Where he spent his childhood. His parent's home. A place he could always come back to. Danny poured water from a bucket into the basin, hung his hat on a peg tacked to the outside plank of the cabin, washed his hands, and splashed water on his face and neck.

The water was brisk. No...it was downright cold. Normally, he would have washed up inside with water warmed in a kettle on the wood stove. But he needed a shock to the system. The water did the trick, awakening his senses, and making him aware of the fact that the journey west might be much easier than telling his parents of his plans.

Danny opened the front door, wholly expecting his father to levy a sizeable lecture on the danger of pursuing golden dreams. But he wasn't there. All was quiet. Danny went to his small room, changed his clothes, and thought about how he was to approach the subject. It wouldn't be easy. His father will probably be disapproving and disappointed in his choice. And his mother was bound to be heartbroken. To satisfy his desire for adventure meant denying his parents a son, at least for a while.

He could hear plates and pots clinking together as they were set down on the fine wooden table where he ate almost every meal of his nineteen years. Danny also heard the legs of wooden chairs as they were pulled back; the voices of Seth, his father, and his mother blended in the type of normal conversation played out day in and day out by innumerable families across the nation.

"Danny, supper is ready." His mother's words snapped him out of his daydream.

"Coming...I...I'm just changing and I'll be there in a moment," Danny answered, a cool sweat forming on his brow.

And now was the moment of truth. He left his room with as much confidence as he could muster, fully expecting to be met by an onslaught of opposition and denouncement. But there was none. There was no mention of the topic at all by his mother, father, or brother, despite the feeling by Danny that there was a thick atmosphere that hung throughout the room. Either Joseph Vance warned off his wife and youngest son, Danny was overly sensitive about the topic, or there was a mixture of both conditions.

In the best way he could, Danny sat down with his family for supper, nervously accepting the ladle full of hearty beef stew and a slice of freshly baked bread. The smell of the food wafted out of the house throughout the afternoon; a mixture of smells that were a constant unconscious reminder of home and security. This was something he never realized until that moment. The prospect of being without has a way of jarring a person into examining what is, and what was, and what may not be.

It's a difficult thing to hide that there is something on your mind with a light sheen of sweat covering your body and the anxious body language that becomes awkward, if not apparent, by all involved. Danny was physically there for supper, but he was far from there. The conversation continued across the table. Danny remained oblivious.

"All I'm saying, ma," sixteen-year-old Seth playfully argued, "is that it'd be nice to go to the dance in town. All the guys are going! There'll be food and music..."

"And girls!" Caroline Vance interjected. "That isn't what you need to focus on young man. Right now, the most important thing for you to do is get an education and help your father and brother. There'll be time enough for the ladies in the future. No time for temptation."

Danny took a shallow breath as if to speak, but the words didn't come.

"Listen to your mother, son," Joseph added. "She knows the evils of women," he wryly added and then half-heartedly dodged the playful slap on his arm delivered by Caroline.

"A boy...might I add...I'm almost a man...a man that needs to have a little fun now and then. You and Pa could go, too! Eat somebody else's food, see some old friends, and kick up your heels. It's a perfect time to say goodbye to Old Man Winter and hello to Sweet Spring! What's the worst that could happen?"

Danny tried again, to no avail.

"Seth, your ma has a good point. You might meet a real harpy who'll steal you away. She just wants to protect you from the corrupting ways and charm of the weaker sex," Joseph stated, knowing that was not what Caroline truly meant. She rolled her eyes and shook her head in disbelief.

His heart was beating faster. It's now or never. Do or die. No time like the present. Danny generates the momentum to speak, but his worry wins. The internal battle once again results in a stalemate.

"Why...I'm my own person," Seth interjects. "There's no harm in having a little fun. How am I supposed to make new friends? Right now, my closest friends are those oxen! Sure, I get to see my friends at school. But this is going to be an opportunity to be around others without a slate in my hands. Besides...nobody, let alone a woman, is going to steal me away. I may steal a little kiss from some lass, though," Seth snuck in with a wry smile and a little wink.

"Oh, my ears!" Caroline screeched in her best, but obviously feigned, offended tone. "You evil young man. I cannot even begin to believe that my sweet son has such bad intentions."

Danny wasn't paying any attention to the debate at hand. All he was aware of was his disgust in himself. His spoon poked at his food, and what he didn't say was more noticeable than he thought. With much consternation, Danny realized that he couldn't tell his parents.

"You're breaking your mother's heart, Seth," Joseph stated with much drama. "Mother knows what is best for you. She knows a little something about those dances. The fact is...that's where we met!"

Caroline buried her face in her hands, seconds before she and Joseph broke out into laughter. Seth, once he caught on to the joke, also chimed in with laughter. It was a chorus of hilarity at the expense of mother and son. The merriment continued for a good half a minute. Everyone got a good deal of enjoyment out of the moment. Everyone, that is, except for Danny. As the laughter died down silence dominated the room. All three members of the family stared at Danny. What was a painful internal struggle for Danny was now a painfully awkward, and inescapable, predicament.

Joseph, in his characteristically no-nonsense way, set eyes with Danny and demanded, "Dammit, boy! Out with it! You've been trying to say something ever since you sat down. I suspect I know what it is. Come on...say it."

Never had Danny been in such a situation. There was no way out except forward. At that moment, sailing around Cape Horn with its violent seas and storms with rain, hail, snow, and waves as big as buildings was preferable to this situation. He created this gathering storm himself, and he felt as if he was facing it in a row boat.

"Pa...Ma," Danny began most uncomfortably. He gripped the edge of the table to steady himself; to calm his nerves and remain focused. "Please...listen to what I have to say. Hear me out and keep an open mind."

He began to relay the information that Stephen gave him earlier in the day. The discovery of gold, the rush of opportunists, the different routes to California, and his and Stephen's decision to strike out overland in a few months. Their faces went from downright grim, to amused, and then interested in what was relayed. This was a difficult thing for his parents, especially his mother. In no way did they want to lose their son. But in no way did they want to hinder his desire to become a man and stand on his own. He was nineteen. Smart, but no scholar. He wasn't going to continue his education at a university back East. And he didn't have a piece of land readily available for himself to scratch out a living. Of course, he could buy a piece of land, but that'd take money—more money than he currently had at his disposal. His reality for the foreseeable future was this homestead, with his parents and his brother. Caroline and Joseph understood this. And even though it hurt inside, and they had their doubts, they knew they had to let him go or face the potential resentment from their oldest son for what could have been.

Caroline got up from the table and walked to Danny. Her eyes were misty, and she showed great strength holding in the sobs that wanted to tumble out of her soul. She grasped the top of Danny's right wrist and hand, bent down, and kissed him on the forehead. "I trust in you, Daniel...I trust in you." That was all she needed to say. That was all she could say. She walked away from the table and into the room she shared with her husband, dabbing her eyes with her apron as she closed the door.

That left Danny, his father, and Seth at the table. Seth knew better than to give his two cents at that moment.

It was better to watch and wait for his father's response. Danny, feeling more confident with his mother's support, also watched and waited. Nervously, he broke off a piece of bread and placed it in his mouth, savoring the warm, yeasty flavor.

Joseph leaned back in his chair and pulled a clay pipe and a small pouch of tobacco from his pocket. Using the bowl of the pipe, he scooped tobacco from the pouch and tamped it down with his thumb. This was Joseph's post-supper routine. Danny tried to read the situation, unsure of its direction. Support or disdain. A flip of a coin seemed more certain in its outcome. Joseph stood up and walked to the cooking stove. He opened the stove and lit a punk. As he turned and slowly walked back to his chair, Joseph held the punk to the bowl, puffed on the pipe stem, and walked through the small clouds of tobacco smoke. Joseph sat down, the pipe between his lips. He snuffed out the punk and tossed it on the table. All the while, Danny waited.

"Boy," Joseph calmly said as he removed the pipe from his mouth and held it in his left hand, "you are an enterprising young man, but you are a fool." He drew smoke through the pipe and Danny felt his heart sink.

"But Pa," Danny began to protest. Joseph held up his hand, signaling Danny to stop in his tracks.

"You're a fool...but you are a fool in the mold of your father. I was like you in my younger days. Full of dreams and desires. Notions that my father disapproved of. I, too, faced a tempest telling my folks I wanted to marry your mother and start a new life in the wilderness. My mother cried, and my father lectured me and did his best to convince me that my fortunes were brighter at home. But I was adamant, and they relented...reluctantly, I must say...but they gave their blessing." Joseph intermittently drew from the pipe, each exhalation of billowing smoke easing Danny, burning away the anxiety that had built up over the last few hours.

"Maybe this is just the thing you need," Joseph continued. "Perhaps you will find a fortune. Hell, I don't know! But at the very least...you may just find yourself; find out what you're made of and what type of man you want to be in this world."

Joseph slowly stood and walked over to the fireplace, tapped the remaining ashes into his hand, and tossed them into the fire. "Son, you've got a lot to think about," he said with a slight smile on his face.

Left alone at the table, Danny sat there, reviewing the discussion that had just occurred. He measured his father's words carefully, somewhat astounded that his father placed the decision squarely within his own hands. It was quite the predicament. On the one hand, he was excited that his father didn't refuse to give his blessing. But a degree of relief would have eased the situation if his father had just said no. Being an adult apparently had its disadvantages.

Leaving the table and retiring to his room, Danny readied himself for bed, but sleep didn't come easily. Heady decisions have a way of keeping the mind occupied when one wants to slip off to slumber. Thoughts of adventure and independence, and the endeavor with his friend, tumbled from one thought to the next, all tinged with flakes of gold. He had to...he just had to go. Danny could always come home. As Danny struggled with consciousness, his thoughts vacillated between what he needed to do to prepare for the trip and home. The mental tug of war continued for what felt like hours until he drifted off to sleep in mid-thought.

Chapter 3
A Trip Delayed

———◆·◆·◆——

U p before the sun, Danny began his day like any other day in his recent memory. Chickens needed to be fed and eggs collected, hogs had to be slopped and tended to, and the dairy cow needed to be milked. There was wood to be split and stacked. And a sundry of other chores, large and small, and mostly monotonous, were completed day in and day out. Added to that was the seasonal work—plowing the land for wheat, corn, and potatoes; harvesting crops; mending fences; fattening up hogs, preparing the meat of any animal slaughtered, and then preserving the meat in the smokehouse. Even dividing the work between his father and brother, there was always something to do.

With the decision made, Danny now sought to balance his responsibilities on his family's farm with his need to earn extra money to fund his trip to California. It was one thing for his father to not deny Danny the opportunity, but it was wholly another for him to think that his father would help pay for the journey or let Danny avoid his obligations on the farm to earn money. He would have to find a way to do it on his own, on his own time, and as quickly as he could. If the goal was to leave before summer arrived, that didn't leave Danny a great deal of time. Every day he was delayed, more men headed west; more claims were staked; more opportunities were lost; and an increasing amount of potential wealth was parlayed to another.

So, that first day he began to think over his situation. Perhaps his timing couldn't be too much better. As winter was coming to an end, farmers and townspeople would have all sorts of projects that could use an extra hand or two. With any luck, the contacts he and Stephen had in the community could be fruitful.

Later that morning, Stephen came by the Vance place to find out the verdict...whether Danny was sentenced to a lifetime of drudgery on the farm, or if he was pardoned to the West. Danny relayed the discussion from the previous evening and was jubilant, if not somewhat shocked, with the fact that Mr. Vance didn't firmly deny Danny's dream. They talked over their desire to leave no later than the beginning of summer, and they concluded that their quest for extra work needed to start as soon as possible. Both Stephen and Danny agreed to find odd jobs, preferably in the afternoons or on Saturdays.

Several jobs were found rather quickly, and the young men set into a pattern of life that was quite demanding. Up with the sun, chores completed, and breakfast eaten. More chores on the farmstead, and then in the afternoon Danny took leave of his family, met up with Stephen, and spent several hours in labor for others. There was always wood to cut. During the winter, large oak, walnut, hickory, and many other types of tree branches broke off...sometimes whole trees came down. In other instances, trees needed to be cleared from a plot of land. Even if they wanted, the boys couldn't keep count of the number of their axe swings. Nor could they keep track of the number of times they pulled on a buck saw or a two-man crosscut saw. Small piles of rounds turned into stacks of wood. Stacks of wood soon turned into cords of wood. Cords of wood turned into income. Each dollar earned came at the cost of free time and rough hands populated with blisters.

When they weren't cutting, splitting, and stacking wood other projects came their way. About three miles from the Vance place, Mr. Johns was making renovations to his cabin. Danny and Stephen were in no way trained carpenters, but they were good at following instructions and were young and full of eager muscle that could help get the job done. Mr. Johns wanted to place a glass pane in the window he had covered with oiled paper. His mortared, rock chimney needed repair. There was also a section of his roof that needed new shingles, which meant removing the old shingles, cutting a shake bolt from a round, and then using wedges and a wooden mallet to cut a new shingle—over and over until dozens were shaved from the block. He also wanted a couple of dormers and a plank floor added to the rafters of his cabin to make a sleeping loft for his children. It was laborious and time-consuming, but it made some money.

Widow Burke, a neighbor closer to Stephen's home than Danny's, needed another chicken coop. As with other farmsteads, the Burke place depended on chickens for meat, eggs, and extra income. This was even more the case for Mrs. Burke, what with her husband gone. She wasn't farming the land. Luckily, she was able to let out her forty acres to a neighbor. With no children, her expenses were relatively small, but they were expenses nonetheless. So, she raised chickens. She supplied eggs to a few neighbors, and Mr. Stapleton's mercantile. Demand for her eggs increased, and in response to the pressure of supply and demand, Mrs. Burke looked to expand. Enter Danny and Stephen. Their carpentry skills were either improving or they had a knack for building a chicken house, which was just a house with creature comforts chickens would embrace. They constructed a structure eight feet by eight feet, and it was between six and seven feet tall. Essentially, inside the coop were two levels with shelves for nesting hens. The roof, high in the front and gently sloping to the back, was covered in thin shingles. A door in the front allowed access into the coop, albeit a tall person would have to stoop to maneuver within its confines. The outside walls, competently constructed of milled pine, made for a tidy appearance of the chicken shack. The boys even added leather-hinged horizontal doors on the sides of the coop to provide easier access to eggs. Proud of their efforts, Danny and Stephen collected their wages and moved on to the next project. Widow Burke was a happy customer, and word of what the boys were capable of doing began to spread. Their chicken coop, for a time, was a popular topic in some quarters. Mr. Vance even had Danny build a similar house at home but without wages rendered for service. It was a chore.

Fences were mended, replaced, and constructed; post-holes were dug, logs split into rails, and rails either nailed into place, wedged into place, or ran through holes bored through posts. Several times, Mr. Stapleton had the boys into town to unload large spring shipments of seed, tools, fabric, and every sort of diverse items that a small town mercantile would carry. Stapleton also employed the boys on occasion to deliver goods to farms in the surrounding area, which played into the search for additional jobs. As the boys unloaded an order, they noted potential work that could be done, quietly discussed if they thought they could do the work and how much they would charge, and then pitched the job to the residents. Some of the men they asked for had no intention of giving them work...perhaps it was pride, or perhaps it was the frugal nature of men try-ing to gain ground on expenses. But many other men saw that the benefit of getting a chore done at a low cost, all the while freeing up time to do something else, outweighed the financial cost.

And the cycle continued, alternating between daily chores and work throughout the community. It wasn't an easy thing. The boys couldn't work every day, or even for long hours due to family obligations. However, they began to feel more confident in their chances of actually earning the funds they needed. Danny reviewed his finances every week, partly as a motivator to keep working toward the prize, and partly to parse out expenses in his head that could be covered. His father, despite his best efforts to hide his feelings, also grew more interested in Danny's progress. At times, Danny could swear that his father beamed with veiled pride. Of course, Mr. Vance tried not to be too supportive, but his restraint steadily wavered a bit each week.

"Danny boy?" Joseph Vance inquired one late spring morning. The air was still crisp, and the morning dew was everywhere evident. As the mornings stretched into midday, however, the sun warmed the earth; the world tripped into the rebirth that only comes with spring.

"Do you reckon you'll be on your way to California soon? Talk down at Stapleton's is that men...and some women and families...from all over the world are trickling in."

Danny thought that it was a peculiar question for his father to ask, seeing as though his father thought going was a foolish proposition to begin with. But the tone in the elder Vance's voice was different than normal. It hinted at concern, maybe even urgency.

"I think we're going to make it...earn enough money, that is. Getting to California might be a different story," Danny replied, a bit puzzled as to the direction of the conversation.

"Naw, son," his father punctuated his statement with a drink of cold water from a ladle dipped into a bucket. "I suspect that if you and Stephen can bust your humps to earn the funds to outfit the trip...you'll make it to California."

He paused, tossed the ladle back into the bucket, and ended the conversation as mysteriously as it began.

"You'll make it...You're a branch none too weak....Now, whether you find what you go there for is hard to say. You'll find something...even if it's the unexpected."

Mr. Vance winked at Danny, then ambled off to the barn to stow some tools.

Make it? A statement of confidence from his father? Find the unexpected? Danny hoped to find out what his father meant by his words and the point of the conversation in the first place. He speculated that if his father was a younger man with flexible responsibilities, then he, too, would head to the gold fields. Since that wasn't the fact, though, he concluded that his father intended to live vicariously through the wanderlust of his eldest son.

The days, as endless as they seemed, trickled into weeks; weeks piled into months; and the passing months were a nagging reminder of the funds still not earned and the urgency of leaving within a reasonable amount of time. It was now May of 1849. Daniel and Stephen set mid-June as the latest that they could realistically leave to avoid the threat of snow in the Rockies, as well as the Sierra Nevada Mountains. Mentally and physically, they were ready. Logistically and financially was another story altogether. Between the labors of the two, Danny and Stephen accumulated close to $170 each. As news from California reached the Eastern ports and spread like fingers across the land, tales...unbelievable tales...continued to feed the frenzy of gold fever. Men finding a hat-full of gold in two hours; fifty-two pounds of gold in eight days; men digging as much as $75,000 worth of gold in that first summer of 1848. Their combined $340 was a paltry amount compared to the wealth reported and talked about in the civilized world. But it was now or never. To delay their trip further meant waiting until the spring of 1850. They couldn't let that happen.

***

It was a Tuesday morning in June, and the day broke warm with a hint of humidity in the air. The kind of day where the moisture in the air combined with smells on the farm to arouse the senses to the point of overload—the animals, the sweet grass, the smell of food...the rugged smell of the earth. The unmistakable smell of home.

Danny had been awake for several hours. Trepidation over the trip, thoughts of what might never be, and acknowledgment that he may never see his family again were a recipe for a restless night of sleep. Sure, he was nervous about the next six months of travel. He was also anxious that the streams and creeks and hills would be played out by the time he crossed the continent. But what gnawed at him through the night were the periodic pangs. Not a physical pain. It was an emotional hurt. A hunger for his family; a hunger that wasn't for *what is*, but for *what will be*. A loss that hasn't happened, although inevitable, solidified with a soon-to-be farewell. He loved his family. They were a place of comfort for him; a warm blanket on a cold morning. This would be a wound that would never quite heal.

Danny got up, dressed, and joined his brother one last time to complete the morning chores. It was bittersweet. Seth was quiet and didn't pay much attention to his older brother. It wasn't out of envy, spite, or hatred...it was his way of dealing with pain and loss. This was his brother, a willing combatant at times, a friend at others; his brother always. So, it wasn't just Danny who was suffering.

In the kitchen, Danny's mother, wearing a plain dress, her hair bundled on top of her head and held with pins, focused on preparing breakfast, not completely pushing aside her anguish over Danny going away. Her Danny...her firstborn. Nobody would taste the tears in the coffee, bacon, biscuits, or eggs.

The only member of the family who wasn't evidently suffering from the soon-to-be separation was Danny's father. Oh, he was sad, but he was more proud of his son than anything else. Sure, at the beginning of this quest, he thought Danny and Stephen were out of their minds and foolish; that this was all for naught and would eventually taper off into just a thought and not action. However, as the months went by and he witnessed these young men and their determination to pay their way, he couldn't help but become an advocate. There will be an empty place within him, and he will worry over his son's plight, but there is a pride he has in Danny. His son set his mind to a task...a goal. He pushed himself toward that opportunity. He was on his way to move mountains. Danny was his father's son.

Stephen would be there soon, after his goodbyes and tears. The boys were lucky in the sense that Stephen had a horse of his own. A dependable beast, the horse was harnessed to an old buckboard wagon Stephen's grandfather allowed him to have and fix. The wagon enabled them to stow a good portion of their gear, but in no way could they transport all that was needed on the flatbed of the wagon. In fact, all they counted on bringing from home were their necessities—bedrolls, eating and cooking utensils, several sets of clothing for warm and cold weather (packed in a wooden chest), an extra pair of boots for each young man, a tent they planned to share, candles, and some tools they could use along the way and in the goldfields (two shovels, two picks, two wooden mallets, two axes, and one crosscut saw). They also acquired a sheet of rubber-backed canvas that had multiple uses, but they intended to use it as a cover for their supplies on the wagon.

Once they loaded the wagon, the plan was to travel to St. Joseph, Missouri, and with any luck, buy into a joint stock company. Stephen heard at Stapleton's that buying into a company was something that many a traveler did. It was more cost-effective to pool funds and purchase supplies, especially provisions. To purchase the hundreds of pounds of food necessary for two people to cross the continent was cost-prohibitive. Buying in bulk reduces the overall price, and the only way to buy in bulk is to have a greater amount of money than was available to Danny and Stephen. So, once they reached St. Joseph the first order of business was to find the right group of folks who would take them in.

Daniel Vance, on the cusp of twenty years old, has never been away from home, let alone across the continent in a strange land. Eighteen hundred miles across plains, creeks, rivers, mountains, and deserts; over three million steps. And the journey begins with what may be the most difficult step of all...the step away from home.

Breakfast was eaten with light conversation; the topic of leaving was avoided by all. Local gossip from Stapleton's, the changing weather, the girls Seth was sweet on...any topic they could muster without the obvious topic at hand. Unsurprisingly, time couldn't be stopped or delayed. The family finished their meal and helped Mrs. Vance clear the table and clean the dishes, a task that was seldom done by the boys. Perhaps it was out of consideration for what their mother was going through, or maybe Danny and Seth were making a feeble attempt to extend their time together. The sound of Stephen's horse-drawn buckboard wagon pulling into the yard jarred the family back to reality. It was time...time for Danny to load up his belongings; time for the journey to begin; time to say goodbye.

"Let me give you a hand with your trunk, Danny," Seth said as he placed the cleaned and dried plate on the table.

"Thanks," Danny said as they walked into their room. With each boy holding a leather handle, they negotiated the doorway, crossed the small common area of the house to the front door, opened the door, and then stepped into the yard to the buckboard wagon.

"Mornin' partner...Seth, Mr. Vance...good day Mrs. Vance," Stephen alternately nodded his head and greeted each person in turn, removing his hat with his gesture to Mrs. Vance. The buckboard, although small, was efficiently loaded and had room to spare, a fact that could be advantageous when joining a company heading west. Danny's trunk was loaded onto the wagon, as were a few tools and odds and ends.

Mrs. Vance didn't leave the house. She just stood in the doorway, watching the boys load their gear. Danny walked to the door and entered the house with his mother. They were out of sight of the others, alone with their emotions.

"Ma...," Danny began but was interrupted by his mother's "shhhhhh."

Her eyes were misty, moisture pooling up at the corners of her eyes, and then rolling down her face. It's a predicament that every parent faces at one time or another. The sound of children running, playing, and arguing becomes the center of the universe for a parent, especially a mother. But those children grow up. They fall in love. They leave. Most offspring might move into a home on the family plot, or to an adjoining farmstead. Maybe they move a few miles away. Danny may as well be moving to another planet as far as Caroline Vance was concerned.

"Please don't say anything," she managed to say. "I know you'll be safe. I know you feel like you have to do this, and if you didn't...well, the regret would eat at you."

Her words were punctuated by soft sobs and periodic dabs at her tears with the white apron that she wore.

"But son, please know that you are always here...in your mother's heart. That's all I have to say. I love you, Danny."

They embraced. Danny felt his mother crying as he hugged her as tightly as he dared. The sound of her crying and the pouring out of her grief was contagious; Danny began to cry, too. After what seemed minutes, Danny wiped his tears away with the long sleeves of his shirt. He kissed his mother's cheek and walked to the door. Before he exited the house, he turned and said, "I love you, ma."

It wasn't hard to see that Danny had been crying, but nobody could blame him. Stephen did the same as he left his home. There was no shame in crying. Red, watery eyes were a badge of love; a proof of humanity. Things would be different with his brother and father, though. The young men were setting off as men. Mr. Vance and Seth, sad as they were, were also excited for this new start in life. If they couldn't venture on to California, then they could live the fantasy through Danny and Stephen.

"Danny...I...I want you to have something to remind you of me," Seth said, slightly out of breath, partly from the physical exertion of loading and shifting items in the wagon, and partly out of the anticipation of his overture.

Seth jogged to the barn and returned to Danny with a small haversack and an item wrapped in an old wool blanket. He set the haversack down, causing a small puff of dust to spring from the outside of the bag and quickly drift away in the slight breeze. The sack held powder, shot, and percussion caps. Seth unrolled the secreted item, revealing the fowling-piece that he and Danny shared on many a hunting excursion. They both received it from their parents as a Christmas gift several years back. Seth had a large smile on his face, beaming happiness at gifting the shotgun to his brother, even though half of it was technically Danny's anyway. The gesture was heartfelt and wholly appreciated by Danny.

"I can't take that," Danny weakly protested, suddenly realizing the benefit of having a weapon along to help procure game, and to protect property and life.

"Just you never mind that big brother...you can repay me when you get back with all that gold! Then you can buy me something new," Seth laughed as his master plan unfolded.

"It's a deal," Danny said as he shook Seth's hand and pulled him in close for a hearty hug and slap on the back.

All that was left in the ritual was a farewell to his father. They stood in front of each other, Danny as tall and as broad as his father. Danny really didn't know how to feel or how to act. He wanted to hug his father; shake his hand; say goodbye like a man; run away; and just get it over with. But where to begin? To begin was to acknowledge, and to acknowledge took a strength that Danny wasn't sure that he had. Luckily, his father had strength enough for both of them.

"Danny, my boy...I'm so proud of you. You, too, Stephen," he proudly stated, looking from Danny to Stephen.

"Both of you set to accomplish a goal. You have a dream, and you've worked hard just to get at that dream. It's only just begun...and it's gonna be hard. But you boys can do anything you set your minds to."

"Watch out for each other, try to avoid trouble, and sinning, and generally just straying from who you are and who you're meant to be."

Mr. Vance stepped toward Stephen, grasped his hand, and wished him the best of luck. And then he turned to Danny and put one of his well-muscled arms around the boy's shoulders. They walked a few paces away from the wagon, for a bit of privacy, where they could speak with a degree of confidence.

"I've meant all that I've said Danny," Joseph Vance spoke in a quiet, calm tone. "I want you to leave here knowing that you are loved and that both your ma and I are so, so proud of you."

Joseph's voice cracked a bit with emotion, but he maintained his strength, albeit the fact that Danny could see the mist in his father's eyes.

"Just remember this...you can leave here...you can wander the wilderness...you can set roots deep in another land...but Danny, you'll always have a home here. The door is always open."

Joseph pulled his son in and embraced him. Father and son, on the precipice of change, whether they liked it or not. They didn't cry, outwardly. There was pain, interestingly enough, though, that embrace transferred a degree of strength and confidence to Danny. He felt empowered and ready to conquer the world, or at least the West. Their embrace ended and they grasped each other's right hand, like men, squeezed, and shook hands like they meant it.

They all, once again, gathered around the wagon as Danny and Stephen prepared to mount up. In a moment of revelation, Joseph almost forgot his parting gift to Joseph.

"Hold on a moment," Joseph said to Danny, and he trotted around the corner of the family's home. A few moments later Joseph returned with a cloth-covered boxy item. Danny wondered what in the world it could be. Mr. Vance set it down in a space on the buckboard. He took a paper-wrapped package from the top of the box-like item.

"This is from your ma," as he handed it to Danny.

Danny wasted no time opening it, revealing a handsome calico shirt that his mother made for her son.

"Your ma thought you might find the occasion to wear this sometime in California. She would have given it to you herself, but...you know."

Danny was touched. Somehow, during the previous months, Danny's mother bought the fabric and worked on stitching that shirt.

"Please tell her that it is a grand shirt and that I said thank you," Danny commented to his pa as he placed the shirt, carefully re-wrapped in the paper, into his wooden trunk with his other personal items.

"And this," Joseph said as he placed his calloused hands on the cloth-draped box, "this is my gift to you."

He slowly and carefully uncovered the box, which wasn't a box at all. It was more like a cage constructed of wood. Inside the cage was a bed of straw. And right there in front of a very confused Danny, and Stephen for that matter, were two laying hens of the Rhode Island Red variety. For a brief second, Danny stared at the hens, and the hens returned the inquisitive gaze, heads cocked while they emitted soft clucks.

Pointing at the larger of the two hens, Joseph stated, "That one there's Penny, and the smaller one is Betsy."

"Well...uh, thanks Pa," Danny said to his father, trying to muster enthusiasm, or at least feign appreciation. "I'm not sure if we have room for these fine-looking girls."

"Seems to me," Joseph replied with a touch of a smile on his face, "it'll fit nicely right where it's sitting. Why, I even got you some feed, but they'll forage well enough if you turn them out on occasion. There's nothing like a fresh egg when you're hungry!"

Pa had a good point, and Danny felt a tinge of guilt for viewing the hens as more of a burden than a gift, but what can you do? Your father gives you a gift (a practical gift in most situations), so you take said gift.

"Fresh eggs will be a treat...I do appreciate the girls, Pa."

The remaining items were secured on the wagon, and the two soon-to-be Argonauts climbed aboard. Their time had come, and it was now or never. Stephen gave a quick flick of the reins in his hands, and the wagon moved forward with a sharp jerk that leveled off to forward momentum. They rolled out of the yard waving their hats to Joseph and Seth Vance. Danny spied his mother in the doorway of the house, dabbing at the corner of her eyes. She waved demurely as the wagon carried the boys and their supplies toward their future. Danny blew her a kiss.

Stephen looked at Danny as the Vance farm disappeared from their sight.

"Chickens?" Stephen asked and exclaimed.

Danny didn't say anything, opting to shrug his shoulders and shake his head.

The two hens, riding unceremoniously in the back of the wagon, continued their chorus of clucks.

Chapter 4
Waiting To Jump

————••◆••————

There were several jumping-off points that the boys could have journeyed to in Missouri—Independence, Westport, Platte City, Weston—but they chose to travel to St. Joseph, a town that was much closer to their home; seven days travel to be exact. Each day was like the previous day. Depending on the terrain, they either both rode on the wagon, one boy would walk, or they would both walk—one leading the horse-drawn wagon, the other pushing the wagon from behind. This was a bit more work than they anticipated, and they were using roads that were maintained. It was a dose of reality that forced them to recognize that they needed more than just one horse to pull their load. But that was a problem they'd deal with when they reached St. Joseph. Until then, they plugged along, sweating by day, setting up camp at night.

As the distance to St. Joseph became less each day, the roads became more congested. What began as two young men, a horse, and a wagon, was within days multiplied by hundreds. By the time they reached the outskirts of St. Joseph, the sights were beyond what they had heard in Stapleton's store. All around St. Joseph were encampments. Small groups; large groups; men roaming around to and fro, most with a purpose, some just milling about. There were make-shift corrals enclosing oxen, mules, and horses, piles of supplies, wagons, harnesses...every item imaginable. The agents of merchants practiced the art of negotiation with individuals and representatives of joint-stock companies. The problem for Danny and Stephen was now twofold: how do they find a group to join, one that was a good fit and comprised of reputable folks, and how to even begin the search for said group.

As they slowly maneuvered the outer ring of St. Joseph, wiping their eyes from the collective dust that beast and man kicked up as they shuffled along, they took in what they could, but it was a cacophony of sounds and conversations.

"You want $115 for a buckboard? Why, that's highway robbery!" a faceless voice from the crowd exclaimed from somewhere nearby, adding to the plethora of conversations.

"...these gold-washing machines will save you time and effort...the envy of any gold seeker..."

"Get your mules here! Mostly broken, just sixty dollars each..."

Daniel moved closer to Stephen, both to speak without shouting and to better hear him.

"Stephen...I'm not sure what to do," the consternation clear in his voice. There were more people gathered here, in and around St. Joseph than he had ever seen gathered in one place.

"You and me both!" Stephen honestly replied. "Maybe we should just find a place for our rig, then go from there?"

That sounded as good as any idea that they could come up with at the moment, so, they continued on until a patch of ground not occupied was found. They both hopped down from the wagon and chained the wheels. Danny checked on Penny and Betsy, giving them some feed and water, and Stephen gave his horse some oats. Danny climbed onto the bed of the wagon, opened a water-tight chest, and retrieved two biscuits and two strips of jerked beef. He stretched to reach Stephen, passed the items, and then stepped off the buckboard by climbing down the iron-rimmed wheel. As they leaned against the wagon and ate, they watched the new world around them.

After about twenty minutes of observation, the boys began to figure the game out. Outfitters roamed the crowds and streets like barkers, as did their emissaries, calling out the items they offered for sale: "Need a wagon?" "Oxen...mules!" "Camp stoves, tents" and on and on. Routinely, people in the crowd approached the men and began the dance, metaphorically speaking, trying to bargain down the price to stretch their funds. It wasn't surprising to learn that prices around the jumping-off points were greatly inflated. The closer a gold seeker got to the trail heading west, the greater the value placed on the supplies needed. It was supply and demand at its finest; one man's need was another man's profit.

Another thing they learned was how to spot leaders of groups headed to California. Those expecting to travel west alone or in small groups bought in small quantities and paid a premium price. Whereas, large companies benefitted from steep discounts. For instance, there was a difference in purchasing 100 pounds of bacon and 3,000 pounds. Their best chance of buying into a company going west was to approach one of the buyers and ask to join. The worst that could happen was to be turned away. No harm, no foul. If they found a troop to join, then they could possibly negotiate their entry fee. The trick was to find a group that was large enough to provide protection from Indians and gain a discount in the purchase price of supplies, but one that wasn't so large that the potential savings in supplies were negated by the sheer amount of goods needed. Danny and Stephen had a total of $340 to work with, which should be enough to enter into a company. What might help their cause was the fact that they had a wagon already. Even having a horse could be beneficial. The chickens were a debatable plus. Two hens couldn't produce enough eggs at any given time to feed a whole company. In fact, in the seven days of travel to the outskirts of St. Joseph, Danny's hens produced a total of four eggs. It was a nice treat for the boys to have a fried egg with a meal. But to benefit a whole company, Danny would need at least a few dozen hens...a veritable mobile chicken ranch.

So, the only feasible line of action was to take their chances and solicit potential groups. As awkward as it can be, there was no other efficient way. Newspaper advertisements might work, and surely they did for individuals who had the luxury of time.

As one man who appeared to be an agent for a company concluded a transaction for twenty broke mules with one of the multitude of merchants, the boys took their chance. Stephen agreed to try first.

"Hey mister," Stephen called to the man as he jogged to his side as the man was walking away with the merchant, "you taking on any men?"

"Sorry son," the man said as he shook his head, "you're just a bit too late. I've already taken on too many people if you ask me. Keep asking around, though. Someone's bound to have a spot. Good luck."

The man continued to get his mules. A man on a mission, no time for additional small talk and pleasantries.

Feeling dejected, although it was only the first of many disappointments he and Danny would experience,

Stephen walked back to Danny, looking around for other opportunities.

Both Danny and Stephen agreed that they'd take turns approaching crew leaders and representatives. But over and over the results were relatively the same. Too many men here; only taking in men from Michigan or Indiana; asking too much for the buy-in; the group appeared to be unorganized and too inexperienced; the agent didn't have time enough to talk. It was enough to exasperate the two young men. However, they didn't work months to earn money, set their minds, leave home, and travel to St. Joseph to turn tail and retreat home. They were from gritty stock, not afraid to push themselves through adversity. As the afternoon crept on to dusk small campfires could be seen everywhere. The smell of burning wood and cooking food combined with the chatter of men, laughter, singing, and periodic boisterousness that'd make getting a solid night's rest seemingly impossible. Danny and Stephen sat around their low fire, the coffee pot on a small bed of coals to keep the strong coffee hot. They ate beans and biscuits as they talked about the day, the excitement of arriving, and the failure to find a company to join.

"We'll find something soon," Danny said calmly and quietly to Stephen between bites of beans and a sip of coffee. "It's just one day...one day. No sense in worrying...yet."

Stephen nodded his head in agreement. They finished their simple, but filling, meal, cleaned their plates, and readied themselves for the night. It was too warm for the tent, so, they just spread their bedrolls under the wagon. There wasn't too much of a chance that their gear would be pilfered, more than likely. Any ruckus—shifting gear, creaking boards, added or removed weight—from above on the wagon would immediately send up an alarm. They both turned in, sleeping in their clothes on top of their blankets. The sounds of hundreds of men, and two softly clucking hens, serenaded them as they drifted off to sleep.

***

In the morning, Danny and Stephen set into their new routine. Wake up, start a small fire for coffee and cook some bacon, stow away the bedrolls, feed the chickens, and then do various other personal tasks. The interaction between buyers and sellers of supplies began relatively early in the day. When hopeful Californians are eager to hit the trail there's little time to waste. That didn't upset the boys none; their hunt for a company to join could begin sooner, rather than later.

Unfortunately, the results were the same. Several hours of disappointment cast a cloud of doubt that did nothing to brighten their mood. As the morning slipped into early afternoon, the temperature began to climb. So, in addition to being irritated with the difficulty the two were having, they were also uncomfortable...and a bit sleepy. Stephen climbed up into the buckboard and nestled into a space where he was in a slightly inclined position. Not altogether comfortable, but not so unpleasant that he thought to move. He pulled his slouch hat down over his forehead to shield his eyes in the hopes of catching a short nap. Danny was of the same mind. With most of their gear still on the wagon, there wasn't room enough for both of them. Danny chose to try his hand at leaning against a rear wagon wheel, a wholly unsatisfactory choice. But he stayed in that position, not destined for a nap. Rather, he watched the action around him.

Fate is a strange creature. Some individuals seem to have all of the luck in whatever their endeavor, rarely experiencing failure. Others struggle throughout life only to experience mixed results. Victory, to some, is the only measure of success. The chase—the mid-point from the beginning to the end—is *the* experience; the only true point of the journey. Danny and Stephen wanted to taste victory, and they proved that they had no qualms with working hard, luck or no luck, to achieve their goals. They possessed a passion and the grit to not give up. Being young and enthusiastic, both of the boys yearned for the chase, although feeling desperate to join a group wasn't, in their minds, part of the chase...it was a necessity; a means to an end. Some folks spend their lives looking for opportunities. But an opportunity has a way of showing up at times when it is unexpected like when a nap is in full swing or a thousand-yard stare has set in.

"You there...mind if I enter your camp for a word," a deep voice said, startling Danny. Stephen was still asleep.

Danny never saw the man approach, being busy with a fixed stare on the crowd thirty yards to his left, watching them all and seeing nothing at the same time. With the man's voice, Danny slowly turned his head toward the words at the same time he became conscious that they were aimed at him.

Still surprised by someone approaching him as he was daydreaming, Danny half-stumbled, half-jumped to his feet, and then brushed the dust from his backside. He glanced at Stephen who was still asleep.

"Yes sir...come on in," Danny guardedly spoke, not knowing what the gentleman was after.

The man, over six feet tall, with close-cropped peppered hair and a well-maintained mustache, wore clothing that was typical of a teamster.

"I'm Jim Kinney," he introduced himself as he extended his calloused hand to Danny. "I've heard you boys are lookin' to join a company headin' to California?"

Reality setting in, Danny was beginning to understand that this was the opportunity they were possibly looking for. He stuck out his hand and grasped Jim's, noticing how strong and rough the man's hands were.

"I'm Daniel Vance...we sure are, mister, but the right group hasn't really come our way."

"Please...call me Jim. What's yer partner's name?" he motioned toward the sleeping Stephen.

Somewhat embarrassed, Danny took off his hat and swatted Stephen across the belly with it. Stephen sat up with a start.

"What...what's going on?" Stephen's eyes and head darted around, assessing the perceived danger. Sensing that the presence of the stranger was what precipitated the disruption of his nap, he rolled to his knees, crawled to the side of the wagon, and jumped down.

"Jim...this here's Stephen Pryor," Danny grasped Stephen by the left shoulder as Stephen shook Jim's hand.

"Nice to meet you," a still confused Stephen exchanged pleasantries, "Jim, you say?"

"Yes...name's Jim Kinney. I'm headin' up a mess of men headin' west. We're 'bout full up, but a couple of them locals sellin' goods mentioned you two and how pitiful you seemed. I figured I'd see for myself if we could use your strong backs. Whatcha boys have to offer?"

This here greatly piqued their interest. They spent a day and a half trying to find a group only to repeatedly be turned away. And now, Jim Kinney shows up at their wagon, specifically asking for them. Danny started off the interaction with cautious optimism, a natural reaction when opportunity, in the form of a tall, gruff individual, comes walking into your campsite. But now for the lack of not appearing to be at a disadvantage while negotiating terms, the boys remained calm, all the while churning with anticipation within.

"Well, Jim...Danny and I are hard workers. We have some gear already. We have this here buckboard, and I have my horse."

"I also have two laying hens," Danny moved to the cage to show Jim his Penny and Betsy.

"That's a start, boys... 'cept for them hens. And that horse ain't gonna work. He'd work for scoutin' and runnin' errands, but if'n you join up, I'm gonna pile 'bout 2,000 pounds of supplies on that wagon. You'll need a team of oxen...at least four of 'em."

Danny took off his hat and scratched his head. "How much will that cost?"

"Depends on who you're dealin' with...goin' rate's as much as sixty dollars for each yoke. But I've got a man I've been dealing with who's sold us plenty of teams...he'll only charge forty dollars."

"That's not too bad," Stephen shrugged his shoulders as he and Danny glanced at each other.

"And then there's the buy-in. Usually, it's one hundred dollars each person, but that's on the condition that you buy a buckboard. Well, you've already got one, so there's that. I figure that you both can become a part of my company for sixty dollars each. You'll also need some spare wagon parts—wheels, tongue. I'll also need you boys to be willin' to do odds and ends on the trail."

It sounded like a decent offer that was not too expensive. Jim seemed to be a capable man, and he had what seemed like a preferred status with some of the merchants.

"What ya boys think?"

Danny and Stephen quickly conferenced, thought that it was reasonable, but also thought it was wise to ask about some of the particulars.

"Let's say we join the company. How many are in your party?"

"Assumin' you join, there'll be 46 men. Most of the men are from Ohio, but we have a few from New York and Pennsylvania. There might be a Virginian in there, too. We're well-provisioned...nothin' fancy, but ya won't starve unless you're countin' on those hens to lay you a meal each day," he chuckled with that last comment.

"So, what type of odd jobs do you have in mind for us," Stephen honestly wanted to know.

"That one's a bit tough to answer. For the most part, it'll just be whatever is needed. Gatherin' wood or buffalo chips...helpin' get wagons unstuck when they's stuck...usin' that hoss from time to time to scout...just doin' what needs to be done as a stockholder," Jim spoke with exaggerated pauses between his thoughts as he rubbed his chin.

The boys believed they could find a group that asked less for the buy-in, but they had go fever. Who knows how long it'd be before they found the perfect match? Here, with Jim, was a train preparing to leave as soon as was feasible. And if the rest of the company was as affable as Jim, all should get along. Were they being asked to do more than if they were patient and joined another group? It seemed that way. Expediency, however, was the order of the day.

"Jim, you mind if Stephen and I talk it over for a moment?"

Jim pulled out a plug of tobacco and cut off a small chunk with a jack-knife he had in his pocket. "I'd think you boys foolish if you didn't." He placed the tobacco in his mouth, folded the knife, returned it to his pocket, and closed the plug of tobacco in a small bag that was slipped into his other pocket.

"What do ya think, Danny? Sounds like an acceptable offer to me."

"It's the only offer, Stephen! But I'm ready...I'm afraid to waste any more time. The faster we hit the trail, the sooner we get to California. I hate feeling like that gold is just slipping away from our hands. Let's do it!"

Agreeing that this was their best, and only, option, they discussed the logistics with Jim. In an hour or two Jim would send a man over to retrieve Danny and Stephen, take them to where they could purchase their oxen and extra parts for their buckboard, and then guide them out to the encampment. Once they reached the camp, they'd check in with Jim, turn over their fees to become a member of the joint-stock company, and then settle into preparations. They shook Jim's hand, sealing the contract, and watched Jim walk to a horse tied to a small tree, untie the reigns, climb into the saddle, and then ride away. The boys were excited to be progressing with their plans. A nap was no longer the desired activity. They spent time repacking their buckboard, hitching Stephen's horse to the wagon for what may be the last time, and then waiting for their man to arrive.

Waiting for an opportunity to arrive can be frustrating. Waiting on a known situation can seem agonizingly slow. They checked and rechecked gear. Items on the buckboard were repositioned. Danny checked on the hens and found no eggs to be harvested. Stephen brushed his horse the best he could with it being harnessed. And they waited.

As promised, Jim's man arrived and introduced himself as Charlie Whittaker. A stocky man with a ruddy face, thirty-year-old Charlie stood about five and a half feet tall. After introductions and pleasantries, Charlie raised his thick right arm, pointed, and indicated that they all were going down that road to purchase the livestock and extra wagon parts. Stephen and Danny walked, one on each side of the lead of Stephen's horse. Charlie walked next to Stephen.

Thirty minutes later, after what seemed like a mile of slow walking exasperated by the stop-and-go flow of people and animals in their path, they stopped at the front of a stockyard. Corrals were brimming with oxen, horses, and mules. Nearby businesses, also dealt in livestock, milk cows, goats, and hogs.

Charlie, in a rather high-pitched gnarled voice, yelled over to a group of men who appeared to be getting nowhere in their conversation, "Jonesy! Hey Jonesy...come sell us some teams!" He waved as he shouted, beckoning Jonesy, the proprietor, for immediate, or at least quicker service.

Jonesy raised his hand, as if acknowledging Charlie's presence and desire for attention, continued his back and forth with his current customers, shrugged his shoulders, turned toward Charlie, and walked over to a sure sale. He shouted over his shoulder as he neared Charlie, "Think it over boys."

"What can I do ya for, Charlie?"

"These folks are part of us Ohio Boys. Kinney wants these here boys to get two teams of oxen and some spare parts for their buckboard...a couple of extra wheels, a spare tongue...probably some wagon bows and a cover...an extra axel," he listed the items off while counting on his fingers. Charlie thought for a moment and continued the list, adding "I suppose they'll also need a pair of double trees, a set of wheel locks, a water barrel, and some Schaeffer's 238 Ultra Supreme Moly grease...that is, if'n they have enough funds for all of that."

Stephen and Danny looked at each other. They were unsure how far their combined $280 would take them in this transaction. If they had any luck at all, they would be able to purchase all that they needed, and they'd have some money left over for emergencies. In the best of the worst case scenarios, they could purchase the necessities, and make do without, borrowing items when needed.

Danny rubbed his head, more out of consternation than pain, took a shallow breath, and asked, "Jonesy...if you don't mind me calling you that...what're we looking at here?"

Jonesy, not missing a beat, informed Danny that everyone calls him Jonesy, so many people that few people even knew his first name. He led the boys to a table where he did his accounting. There was one chair, which Jonesy sat in, taking a mostly empty piece of paper to tally up what it would cost to acquire all of the items on their list. Danny and Stephen crowded in as close as they felt was appropriate, eagerly sneaking a peak at Jonesy's computations. Two yokes of oxen, $80; wagon wheels, $25 each; two yokes, $16; extra wagon tongue, $20; spare axel, $75; wagon bows and cover, $45; grease, $2; water casks, $5 each. The boys watched the numbers add up. Without the wheel wrench and wheel locks, the total was $268, a tough pill to swallow when they had $280. Jonesy revealed the damages to them, and both Stephen and Danny were quite disheartened. If they bought everything they supposedly needed, then they would only have $12 to spare—for ferry crossings, emergency supplies, or anything that may require extra funds.

The boys discussed their options, including Charlie to tap into his knowledge. It was possible they could forego the cover for the wagon, still purchase the wooden bows, but use their rubber-backed canvas as a makeshift cover. This would save them forty dollars...allowing them to have emergency funds of fifty-two dollars...a sum that allowed for a more comfortable cushion.

Concluding their purchase, their additional gear was placed in the wagon. The oxen were harnessed in the yokes and then attached to the wagon. Stephen's horse was tied to the back of the buckboard, and the team was awkwardly led toward the Ohio Boy's camp. It was evident that even with their experience of using oxen on the farm to pull a plow or pull stumps, using a team of oxen linked together was a wholly new experience. Both the oxen and the boys would need training. As they neared the camp, Charlie assured the boys he and Kinney would help them learn proper technique, and give them practice before they moved on out.

They arrived and were shown where they could set up their camp. Kinney came by to settle up with the boys, making them full members of the company. Their training would begin in the morning, and Jim would confer with other leaders to decide what company equipment would be assigned to the boy's rig, as well as what their role would be on the way to California. There would be a meeting in the morning and a chance for introductions. Until then, the boys were on their own.

***

Since the company was scheduled for a week of training, the boys decided to do as many others in the company had done. They broke out their tent and set it up, moving their wooden trunks, bedrolls, and personal items into the structure. They also transferred their mess kits, Danny's fowling piece, and Stephen's rifle into their temporary home. It wasn't much of a home—four canvas walls with ridge poles, a dirt floor, two chests that doubled as seats, and some candles to provide light at night. No real beds, and a bare minimum of privacy. But it would shelter the boys from the elements...for the most part. It would suffice for the next week, and it'd be all they had for the next four to six months, maybe even longer.

They built a small fire ring and started a fire to cook their supper in a Dutch oven and boil some coffee in their pot. Their cast iron Dutch oven was a versatile tool, used for frying, baking, sautéing, and storing food. Their coffee pot was nothing special. Stephen poked at strips of frying bacon while Danny searched the makeshift chicken coop to find that his hens produced two eggs. This was a nice surprise considering the hens were very selective as to when they wanted to produce eggs.

Danny stroked the hens and eased them aside to collect his reward. Their excited clucks announced their disapproval, but they abandoned their opposition. He balanced the eggs in his left hand as he closed the clasp of the cage. Before he could return to Stephen, even before he had the chance to remove his hand from the clasp, Danny heard laughter behind him as he felt someone grab his left wrist.

"Lookie here boys! This girl got us some eggs!"

The words tumbled out of the mouth of a tall man with a shaved head. His lips, curled around bad teeth, tossed spittle as he harassed Danny. Behind the man was a gang of three individuals. They all appeared to be street-wise men from a city, not the farm-bred country boy stock Danny and Stephen belonged to. Ruffians and bullies, ran in a pack as they tend to do, choosing to pick on the weak and vulnerable. Usually, the nastiest of the gang was the leader, and the man grasping Danny's wrist appeared to be the head lout.

Danny didn't know what to think about the situation. He'd never laid eyes on these men, and he didn't initially understand their intentions. For most of his life, Danny hadn't met a stranger or exchanged an ill word. Sure, he'd had a few dust-ups with school chums, however, they were nothing more than wrestling matches and rough play. Danny had never been in an actual fight, and he hoped to maintain that record. That potentiality was now largely dependent on the actions of the man standing in front of him.

Caught off guard, Danny looked the man square in the eyes and asked, "What can I help you with, friend?"

The man laughed and looked over his shoulder to his cohorts. "You hear that? He wants to be our friend!"

Danny tried to pull his hand away only to meet resistance. The man's strong grip meant business.

"You've got my eggs," he said, yanking on Danny's arm only to experience resistance of his own.

Stephen, no longer interested in the sizzling bacon, stood up, ready to aid his friend. His movements were countered by one of the members of the gang who stepped toward Stephen. A showdown seemed imminent.

"You're quite mistaken," Danny sharply stated as he violently wrenched his arm from the grasp of the man, which, unfortunately, resulted in both eggs being hurtled to the ground. Almost immediately, the man threw a right hook toward Danny's head, but Danny anticipated the move and blocked it with his right hand. Then Danny rushed the man and hit him squarely in the midsection with his right shoulder. He wrapped his arms around the man, picked him up, and then slammed him to the ground. They rolled around, jostling for advantage.

Stephen's situation wasn't much different. He found himself fists up, walking in a circle with his combatant. They took turns throwing punches at each other, landing glancing blows. The two other men in the gang spread out, looking for the opportunity to jump into the scrum.

Dust was flying, curses were yelled, and a crowd began to gather. As the combatants continued to struggle, Danny and his fight partner rolled away from each other and struggled to their feet. They were covered in dirt and straw and pumped full of adrenaline. The same thing held true for Stephen and the man he was struggling with. As all involved continued to trade punches, the number of people gathered around to witness the spectacle grew. It was cheap entertainment during an otherwise routine day.

The man fighting with Danny hit him in the upper chest, causing Danny to stumble back a few steps. Seeing an opportunity to go on the offense and get the upper hand, the man rushed Danny. Luckily, Danny read the situation correctly and threw the man to the ground, generating a plume of dust, the scattering of small rocks, and a chain of language unsuitable for young ears.

Before Danny could take advantage of the situation he was hit from behind by one of the stray men from the gang. Danny had the breath knocked out of him. The new man grabbed Danny from behind in a bear hug, rendering Danny's arms rather useless. A vulnerable target, Danny resisted the best he could, twisting and turning, attempting to shake away. Given enough time, Danny might have broken loose, especially if Stephen was able to provide some help, but Stephen was tackled to the ground by the spare man on that side and was fending off blows the best he could. Meanwhile, the man Danny threw was on his feet, quickly approaching the restrained Danny.

"Ya think you can stop me? Ya can stop anything I want to do?" the man asked but more exclaimed.

He punched Danny in the stomach, an unexpected blow that sucked the air that remained from Danny's lungs. He slugged Danny again with the same result. The man pulled back his right arm to drive it into Danny's face. Just as he was set to transfer weight forward through his tricep, through his bicep, through his forearm, through his fist, and into Danny's jaw, a pistol shot rang through the chaos. Jim Kinney was standing there, the smoking pistol pointed toward the sky. The combatants, and those not under the control of the gang, stood there, frozen in the moment. It was as if they feared Kinney. Maybe it was respect. Perhaps it was just the fact that Kinney was holding a pistol that had five more shots.

"Those boys are in my company," Kinney angrily shouted at the gang. "Let them alone!"

The man eased his right arm, reached up to the side of Danny's face, and then lightly smacked it twice. "Let 'em go boys." The men let Danny and Stephen go; they stumbled and slipped to the ground.

"I've told ya before, Roberts...get out and stay out of my camp! No more warnings...no more chances! And these boys," Kinney motioned to Danny and Stephen, "they're off limits, just like all of my men. Ya hear?"

"Oh...we hear ya, Kinney," the leader now known as Roberts, said as his men picked up hats and straightened themselves after the tussle.

They confidently walked out of the camp. As they left, Roberts spun on the ball of his left foot so he was now temporarily walking backward. He looked to Danny and Stephen who were on their knees, tired and bleeding. They were staring at Roberts, who gave them a mock salute, and chimed, "I'll see you later, boys...." He laughed as he spun around, jogged up to two of his men, tossed his arms around their shoulders, and walked on. Their hooting and hollering could be heard as they walked away, even over the murmuring of the small crowd that was now on the verge of going back to minding their own business.

Danny and Stephen, coughing and panting, needed a moment to recover. Jim Kinney walked over to the boys and asked, "You boys gonna be alright?"

Stephen raised his hand, palm forward, and worked out the sentence, "We'll be fine...just need to catch our breath...who...who were they?"

"They're the Roberts Boys...just a few ruffians who like to pick on the weak. It's not that they're bigger or faster...but bullies like them fight in a pack. If'n they fought man-to-man, they'd have their hands full. But in a pack, that's another thing altogether. I don't think they'll be a problem for you boys anymore...but watch your back."

Kinney extended his hand and first helped Stephen and then Danny to their feet. The boys thanked Kinney for evening the odds, and Kinney went on his way. The boys brushed the dirt off their clothes the best they could, went back to their now over-cooked bacon, and then sat down to ease their aching bodies. They talked of the fight—what they did and what they should have done. They talked about their schedule for the next day. And they talked of the need for a good night's rest.

After chewing on their less-than-appetizing bacon and mostly edible biscuits, and then chasing it down with piping-hot coffee, they checked on the well-being of the stock and chickens. All was well, except for their new bruises and resentment for the Roberts gang. But anger and resentment, especially at the moment, was wasted energy. If they see the Roberts Boys again, then they could tap into their fury. Otherwise, there was no point. The night enveloped the camp, washing away the light of day and the tension of the fight. They cleaned up and then turned in for the night.

By the light of the candles, Danny spent twenty minutes writing a letter to his mother. He wanted to let her know that they'd reached St. Joseph safely and that they were now members of a company called the Ohio Boys. Danny described all that he'd done so far, the great number of Californians, and when he surmised they'd begin on the Overland Trail. Sparing his mother worry, he left out the tussle with the Roberts Boys. It was a letter, similar to the many he'd write home, to ease the worry his parents may have. In a way, it also served as a connection to the security of his home.

Finished with the letter, Danny set it aside, blew out the candles, and drifted off to sleep.

**

With the new day, there were new routines and experiences. It was their first true step toward California. They were full members of a company, led by a well-respected and capable man. Jim Kinney had much experience as a teamster—a man who made a living packing wagons, stringing teams of oxen, and traveling the land. He had been to the Oregon Country...to the Mormon settlements near the Great Salt Lake...to Santa Fe when under the control of Mexico...and to the string of American military forts throughout the West. Just like the men he was leading, Kinney was bit with gold fever. He was just as anxious to get on the trail, but he also knew he had the responsibility to train his men how to handle teams, pack and unpack their wagons, be responsible for their place in the company, and work and travel as one unit across the continent. He had his work cut out for him.

There were other teamsters in the company, which helped. However, the majority of the company members were ordinary Americans with little to no experience on the trail—farmers, saloon keepers, mechanics, teachers, and doctors. They were city dwellers and farm boys, all with wild dreams of wealth and adventure. Most of the men had no intention to set down roots in California. Rather, they sought to get to the diggings, stake a claim, work the claim until they reaped the wealth they desired, and then come back home to pay off loans, buy a business, buy a farm, get married, or just retire to a life made possible by gold. Big dreams; dreams that required much work and even greater luck.

After a quick breakfast, the whole company turned out for a meeting. Summoned by a bugle, all 46 members made their way to Kinney's wagon to receive orders of the day. Charlie took roll call and confirmed to Kinney that all members were present and accounted for. Satisfied, Kinney climbed into the back of his well-built wagon to gain height over the company and project his voice.

"Men...today we begin a few days of trainin' with your teams. You'll be divided into smaller numbers for your learnin' and drills. Me and Charlie...Brookes and Lane...we'll each take a portion of ya to work with. Listen for your name and report to your man."

In turn, Charlie, Brookes, and Lane climbed into their wagons and took turns with Kinney yelling out names on their list. Danny and Stephen, just like all of the members of the company, quietly waited to be hailed. Apportioning the men to their respective units didn't take too long. As Danny and Stephen heard their names called by the man named Lane, they answered in the affirmative and walked over to Lane's rig. Lane, a man who worked for a time as a teamster under Kinney, was in his early thirties, tall and lean, with a tanned face and blonde hair. He had a friendly disposition, but he was also charged by Kinney to take his job seriously.

Lane introduced himself to his unit and then explained each part of the wagon, and how the oxen were attached to the yoke and attached to the tongue of the wagon. It was an elementary and oversimplified explanation, but Lane wanted to be sure that he didn't neglect to describe anything. The men in his group weren't put off. If anything, they appreciated his attention to detail. Stephen and Danny had some experience working oxen and horses, as did one of the other six men in the unit, but they had no experience working with a team of multiple oxen. Each pair of men, for the company was designed to have two to three men assigned to each wagon, had their turn naming the parts of the wagon and their function, as well as harnessing and unharnessing the team of oxen. Three times the pairs went through the ritual. It was a fairly simple procedure with Lane's team, a team that was docile and used to being worked with.

Lane also demonstrated to the group how to properly control the animals. A rope lead was affixed to the dominant oxen in the front of the team, and the driver used a long stick to direct the oxen...not by whipping the beasts, but by nudging them in the direction the team was supposed to walk. Once they felt confident, the men were told to go back to their camp, break it down, load all of their gear, hitch their teams, drive them to where Lane worked with them, and then set up their camp. The unit would now live near each other and work with each other, as a unit, but also as part of the machinery that functioned as a company.

It was a long day for all involved, but one that was necessary. Each team in each unit of the entire company would
drill for several days. Packing and unpacking. Rigging and
unrigging the teams. Learning to direct the oxen. Within a
day, the unit joined with other units, forming their wagons
into a circle to enclose the oxen and other livestock at
night. They were getting a crash course in being a teamster, a move designed to train a company to be proficient
enough to embark on their journey. What they lacked in
skill, they would acquire on the trail out of practice and
necessity.

Over the next few days, the boys developed bonds with
their new camp-mates—Alexander Lander, brothers Albert and Jeremiah Swanson, David Timmons, and cousins
Brendon and Dennis Connelly. They ate together, maintained a common camp, helped each other make repairs
on their equipment, and generally learned how to coop-
erate as a unit. Luckily, they all had several things in common—they ranged in age from 19 to 35; had experience
as laborers working on farms, in blacksmith shops, as carpenters; and were eager to learn and get on the trail as soon
as feasible.

The unit did learn fast, and they were receptive to suggestions. Within two days, they were handling their teams
with confidence and a degree of skill. On the fourth day,
each unit took turns taking their rig to the company's central cache of supplies. Each unit had one wagon dedicated

as the mess wagon, carrying the cooking gear and the rations needed to feed eight men plus the unit leader. Eating utensils, stools and a small table, a small stove, an extra barrel of water, alcohol, and a spirit stove were essential items packed into the mess. Personal items, once stowed on the now mess wagon, were placed on one of the other wagons of the unit. The remaining wagons of the unit carried a share of the company's provisions and spare parts. Each wagon had its owner's name painted on its canvas cover for easy identification.

Four units in the company. Each unit rolled with four wagons, and on each wagon were approximately 2,000 pounds of essentials. Forty-six men—Californians—were set to leave the following morning. They were leaving their own known world and heading to their destiny. What that destiny turned out to be was the great unknown.

Chapter 5
Forever Walk

———•·•◆•·•———

At four o'clock in the morning, the company bugler sounded off and the camp sprang to life. Tents were taken down, breakfast eaten, teams hitched, and the units lined up two abreast to head toward the Missouri River. This river was the first of many obstacles the company, and every other company had to face on their trek west. They were excited.

Finally, they were working their teams with a destination in mind. How tempting it was to push the teams as fast as they could go. But it would have all been a fruitless effort. The closer they got to the river, the more congestion they experienced. The only real way across the river was to use one of the many ferrying companies in operation. The Ohio Boys lined up to board one of the many scows that shuttled two wagons across the river at a time. They lined up, as did every other company ahead of them. If they expected to cross the Missouri as soon as they reached the expanse of water, they were sorely mistaken. So, it was all about hurry up and wait. Men idled their time away by making adjustments to loads, playing cards, visiting with other companies, and perusing the wares sutlers had on hand. Some men bartered with each other for items they might need or want. Anything to while away the time spent waiting. Danny checked on his hens and fed them, their appreciation shown through a series of soft clucks.

Half of the day was spent waiting for their turn on the ferry service. Eventually, the company paid their toll—six dollars for each wagon—and began to load their teams onto the scows. Paying the toll entitled the use of the scow, and a crew worked to row their passengers and teams across the Missouri, but the passengers were still expected to pitch in and help with the rowing. As the company's teams began to disembark on the other side of the Missouri, they formed up into their assigned units and waited for the full company to arrive. The whole procedure took hours, leaving the company just a few hours to head farther west on the St. Joseph Trail.

Glancing over his shoulder as the team moved on, Danny looked across the river to see team after team piled up, waiting for their turn at the scows. Looking forward as far as could be seen, wagon tracks stretched on and on. It was a testament to the mass exodus to California; innumerable individuals chasing a variety of dreams. At three miles an hour, the company was able to put about six miles between the Missouri River and their current position. As Kinney would do over one hundred times, he gave the order to make camp—making the wagon corral and setting up tents. The cooks for each unit started cooking fires and preparing supper. Others, including Danny and Stephen, traveled down to creek bottoms to gather wood for their fires over the next few days. Despite not making very many miles, the company was thrilled to make some progress.

Over the coming weeks, the pattern of trail life became second nature. The cook for each unit prepared breakfast from stores kept in the mess wagon. While that was being done, other members of the unit broke camp and prepared their teams for travel. Kinney called for the company to head out by having the bugler sound the order, and the train steadily rolled on, mile after mile, toward California.

When climbing steep slopes, the units doubled up teams. The same thing was done when teams were mired in mud. To slow the impact of gravity when going down a steep slope, the back wheels of a wagon were locked with chains. Later in the afternoon, the company stopped and made camp. The make-shift corral was arranged, the stock was turned out, fires were started, and supper was prepared.

During the hours spent in camp, the mess wagons were restocked from the company's supply of provisions, and men tended to washing and mending clothing, writing letters to be sent back home at the next opportunity, reading, hunting for much-desired fresh meat, and just generally doing mundane chores that broke the pattern of walking all day and caring for teams. Some of the time in camp, though, was spent taking care of the sick.

The biggest killer on the trail was not Indians, nor was it gunplay between Californians. It was cholera. Causing extreme cases of diarrhea and the resulting difficulties of dehydration, cholera turned robust, healthy men into dwellers of the ground—dead men. The illness killed rather quickly. A man might feel perfectly fine during the day, but that evening he may be overcome with the sickness. By morning, he may be dead. If it didn't kill a man, his illness lingered on for days, possibly weeks. Ignorant of the causes of cholera, large numbers of Californians drank water or ate food that was contaminated. Wise captains sought out fresh campsites with clear running water, although the greatest precautions often fell short. Some companies were impacted more than others, losing a portion of their members before making it to Fort Kearny. In all, the Ohio Boys lost four men to cholera, men who were buried along the trail with an untold number of other victims. Their lives are briefly summed up by the hastily made grave markers.

As the Ohio Company continued west, they encountered an ever-increasing amount of items along the trail that previous adventurers discarded to lighten loads. All manner of goods found to be less than useful on the trail became free for the taking, assuming the items could be repurposed. Extra wagon parts and yokes could be a god-send. Buckets, ladles, cooking pots, and tools were useful at times. Beds and pianos...not so much. It wasn't un-common for enterprising citizens of St. Joseph, Independence, or any of the numerous towns near jumping-off points in Missouri to take mostly empty buckboards out to the Overland Trail to collect discarded gear. Ironically, discarded gear was often sold to new customers eager to reach California, enriching merchants and entrepreneurs time and again.

A team might find itself lucky to come across a party that has had enough, heading back east to the life they abandoned. These bedraggled travelers were a wealth of information—the dangers on the trail; where the water was good; whether Indians were expected to be seen; and how the grass was in the miles ahead. They could also be counted on to sell their unneeded supplies to recoup some of their cost. No need to haul hundreds of pounds of bacon, coffee, or other staples home when a Californian might be willing to purchase the items at a discounted price. Those who had seen enough of the elephant were also a means to send letters back to family and friends, which Danny and his compatriots took advantage of on several occasions. In all, misfortune could be a benefit to those who pushed on.

The rutted trail, when dry from the scorching sun, was whipped into clouds of dust as wagon wheels, like water

wheels, picked up dirt and tossed it aside with each rev-
olution. Each step Californians took resulted in the same
thing. The majority of Argonauts walked most of the way
to California. It was somewhat a luxury to ride in the wagon, for the extra weight added burden onto the oxen's load.
The only real exception was for individuals who were too
ill to walk. A company could spend days in camp hopefully nursing the ill back to health. However, the delay
could mean danger for all involved. Water could become
spoiled by others. Graze the teams depended on may become scarce. Snow could clog the passes. This meant that
traveling with the sick was often an uncomfortable, but
time-saving, fact of trail life. Every step was a pace closer
to the Sacramento River Valley. It was a chance all were
willing to take.

***

A long, arduous journey is often best tackled by breaking it down into achievable goals. Accomplishing goal
upon goal has a way of whittling away the immensity of a
situation. Californians leaving St. Joseph, Missouri for the
1,800-mile trip to the gold fields, including the Ohio Boys,
set established military outposts as benchmarks. Reach-

ing Ft. Kearny, Ft. Hendricks, and then Ft. Laramie were milestones worthy of moderate celebration. They not only marked progress across the continent (Ft. Kearny was in what would become the state of Nebraska, while Ft. Hendricks and Ft. Laramie were in what would be Wyoming), but they were also little islands of American civilization. Being an extension of the government, forts served as a post for thousands of letters back to the states. They also served as depots that offered items to resupply low stocks or provide creature comforts...if a patron could afford the inflated prices. The farther away one traveled from settled America, to the hinterland, and out onto the frontier, the higher the prices. Scarcity weighed heavily with distance.

As with Californians who gave up on their quest, the forts were repositories of information. Soldiers sent out on patrols, possessed relatively up-to-date information on the trail ahead and the general threat level from Indians in the vicinity, which was typically very low. Typically, the only Indians many of the California-bound ever saw while crossing the Great American Desert were at the forts, where tribes traded for goods or parlayed treaties and agreements.

The forts were a welcome sight for the weary...a reminder of the nation they were temporarily leaving behind. Likewise, the weary served as a connection to home for the soldiers who served in an otherwise isolated and desolate location. It was a short-term coincidence of wants and needs.

If the company wasn't passing through the territory with a purpose, they might feel like tourists on a working vacation. The scenery they encountered was spectacular. On the Great Plains, often referred to as the Great American Desert, the browning sea of grass stretched as far as the eye could see, gently waving with the breeze, interrupted only by the crags, coulees, and ravines that cut across the land, or the number of creeks and rivers that watered the seemingly dry land. The spectacle of Mother Nature was on full display on that expanse of land. From the rising of the sun in the morning to the sunset in the evening that painted the sky a mixture of orange, crimson, and yellow. God's beautiful work was difficult to put into words. For hours the scorching sun punished all in its path, and then the wind picked up and a gathering thunderhead would blow into their vicinity dumping sheets of rain onto the plain, drenching everything. As miserable as it could be, if one closed their eyes and used their sensory memory, they could remember the heat on the skin, the taste of dust in the mouth, and the smell of rain mixed with the earthy fragrance of the dirt and stock animals.

As if the visual charm and fury of nature weren't enough, the animal life was also something to behold. Since the reports of the Lewis and Clarke Expedition, many Americans romanticized the West and what was considered exotic wildlife. The yip-yapping and howling of coyotes, something the majority of easterners had never experienced, inspired awe, as well as raised the hair on the back of one's neck. Many an hour could be easily wasted watching coyote pups at play or solo coyotes mindfully picking steps, ending in a graceful leap to pounce upon a small rodent. One could also be amused by the massive villages of prairie dogs, their interconnected entrances to underground dens allowing the little critters to pop up and disappear at ease. Like little soldiers standing guard, prairie dogs on the outskirts of the village kept a keen eye out for predators, their chirp causing residents to scatter for cover when danger appeared.

If a company was lucky, they might run across a small herd of Pronghorn. Fast runners, but curious animals, men with all manner of firearms might appear to take one of them down. The same thing was true for any mule deer or elk that ventured near. After a month on the trail, the desire for fresh meat motivated the men to hunt, whether it was a pursuit of opportunity or a hunt planned during downtime. As a comparison, the men on the Lewis and Clark Expedition ate an estimated ten pounds of meat a day but longed for fruits and vegetables. Many Californians had the opposite problem.

But the big treat was if a company crossed the path of a herd of bison. Enormous animals, they numbered in the millions across the Plains at this time. The shaggy beasts, weighing as much as 1,400 pounds, were awe-inspiring, especially when bunched up in a herd. A wagon train might be held up for hours waiting for a herd to clear out of its path. The amount of meat a bison provided was impressive, except for the fact that Californians had no real way to keep the meat fresh in the middle of the summer. As soon as an animal was killed it began to deteriorate. Most of the meat had to be cooled before it could be consumed, and with the schedule a company hoped to keep, only cuts of meat that could be immediately eaten—the back strap, heart, liver, and tongue—were typically taken. This was the case with all big game animals unless a company expected to stay in a fixed location for several days. It was wasteful, but a reality of trail life.

***

One early evening, after the company had made a fifteen-mile day, Stephen and Danny sat on some rocks at the edge of a creek. With their boots and socks off, they leaned back, braced their bodies on their hands, and dangled their feet in the cool, slowly moving water. Their feet were sore, so, a good soaking was a welcome retreat. As they sat there, their minds trailed away from the responsibilities of the day, as well as the redundant nature of trail life, and became lost in collective daydreams.

"What do ya 'spose our folks are doin' back home?" Stephen lazily asked Danny.

Danny thought for a moment, scratched his nose, and made his best guess. "It's getting on in the day, so, they're probably finishing up chores...my ma's working on supper...maybe a stew...or maybe fried chicken...."

"Don't you tease me, now!" Stephen shot back, the taste of fresh fried chicken coming back to him as clear as day. "What I wouldn't give for some fried chicken right now! Don't get me wrong...Brenden makes some decent grub. I appreciate what we get, but the variety leaves much to desire. Bacon and biscuit...salt beef and biscuit...bacon and bacon. And the fresh meat we do get...well, it just ain't enough, often enough. Mmm, mmm...fried chicken."

"You best not be thinking of my Penny and Betsy," Danny laughed. "Them's my egg-laying girls...they're not for fryin'."

"I wouldn't think of it...well, not for too long anyway!" Stephen loved to rib his friend, although cooking and consuming those hens did cross his mind, if only for a fleeting moment. "I could really go for some greens."

"Maybe some corn...fresh peas...cabbage. That'd be something else!"

Danny and Stephen sat quietly, salivating with the thought of fresh food from home. The silence wasn't unpleasant; it bound them together.

"My pa's probably putting tools up right now. Seth...that poor boy is building muscle, pulling his and mine weight around the yard." Danny sighed, "I better find my share of gold, and some, or that boy'll whoop me...and I believe he'll be strong enough to do just that."

"On the bright side, Danny, you've been walking so much I bet ya could outrun him!" Both boys had a hearty laugh over that one. Their laughter made them feel less homesick and turned their thoughts toward the future.

"We're gonna stake us a rich claim...dig out a fortune. Just think...every pan...every shovel-full...every yard of dirt we pull...painted with gold...just painted with gold!" Stephen was, perhaps, the more optimistic of the two, but his enthusiasm was contagious. Danny couldn't help but join in.

"That's right, boy! We'll make more money than we'll know what to do with! I'm gonna help my folks; pay their bills and such. Find me a piece of land near my folks...start my own life. Shoot," Danny added, "I'll even buy Seth some land, right next to mine."

"Me...I'll help out my folks, too. But me...," Stephen's eyes had an extra twinkle within, "me...I'll buy a business in town. Maybe an inn or a saloon. Folks always need a place to stay, and always want a drink. The money would roll in...wealth would build wealth."

Just about that time the boys heard the steps of a horse and turned to see Kinney meandering down to the creek. He steered his horse downstream of the boys and stopped. Kinney's horse lowered her head to drink deeply from the flowing water. Kinney took in the early evening sky spanning from the hills to the horizon. Danny and Stephen, always intimidated by the presence of the no-nonsense Kinney, felt the need to acknowledge his presence, but also desired to give him his space.

"Howdy Cap'n," Danny nodded and spoke.

"Evening, boys. Getting some rest in?"

"Yes sir. Feels nice to be off my feet for a bit," replied Stephen.

"Seems like you two are workin' out just fine. Ain't had nary a complaint. Keep it up."

The boys smiled at the compliment. Kinney was the closest thing they had to a father figure out in the wilderness. Praise or displeasure from him weighed heavily with the boys...with most men in the company.

"Cap'n...we're sure anxious to get to California! How much more time do you reckon it'll take?" Danny asked, not trying to sound desperate to arrive.

Kinney gave the reins a little flick to get the horse's attention. Using his boot heels, he lightly poked the horse's sides to move it along. The left side of Kinney's mouth curled into a small smile as he replied, "In time, boys...in time. Rest up, gentlemen, for tomorrow we continue our drive."

He trotted off, leaving the boys wondering just how much time it would take to get to California. That became the predominant thought for at least some time each day.

***

As the miles piled on, every Californian figured that their journey must surely be complete sometime soon. The plains seemed to be endless, rolling on and on. Distant mountain ranges, initially a speck on the horizon, became larger as the days passed. And just like the geography, the distance traveled changed men on the trail. Many became stronger; their constitutions tested, their bodies improved, and their confidence increased. The mundane and redundant tasks performed daily on the trail gave proof to them that they were up to the challenge. It wasn't their past and what they left behind that they constantly obsessed about. It was their future—the potential of the journey. They grew as men.

With many others, though, they began to shrink into themselves. Even though the mountains grew bigger with each step, they moved in the opposite direction. They were driven by *what was*, not by *what could be*. Each step, each hardship, drew their minds back to home; the uncertainty of the future juxtaposed with the consistency of life at home. It could be the endless walking, the lack of variety of food, the uncomfortable sleeping conditions, or the breaking of equipment that could cause a man to snap and abandon the quest for California.

Take, for example, the effort needed to repair a broken spoke on a wagon wheel. If a team had an extra wheel, the effort required jacking the wagon up, using a wheel wrench to remove the lug, removing the wheel and replacing it with a new one, tightening the lug, and then lubricating the mechanism with grease. But if you didn't have a spare, it was necessary for someone in the group—preferably a wheelwright—to have the knowledge and tools required to make the repairs. The metal ring around the wheel needed to be eased off. Once that was done, the wooden wheel could be dismantled to remove the broken spoke. The new spoke, perhaps one that was part of the supplies purchased for the journey, scavenged from broken and discarded wheels along the trail, or manufactured on the spot, was aligned and secured in its proper location. The wheel was now reassembled and then measured to make sure the metal outer ring is the correct circumference. If not, then the metal ring needed to be heated and worked to either increase or decrease its size. Once correct, the slightly smaller ring was heated to expand the metal and then placed around the wooden wheel where it would shrink when cooled, and be a snug fit. That is a time-consuming process. To do it once could be frustrating. A team with multiple breakdowns might feel differently about continuing.

Danny and Stephen progressed from boys to men. Sure, they were still referred to as boys by the older men of the company, but they pulled their weight and then some. When wood was available, they helped gather a supply for their unit and helped other units when they could. When wagons became mired in mud, they helped push and pull the rigs free. They shared any game they killed, aided in herding livestock, took their turn on watch, and were genuinely good members of the company. This endeavor was a challenge to them; something they relished and took as a rite of passage. Every struggle and sacrifice, all of the misery they endured, was part of the journey they embraced.

***

For a little over a month, the Ohio Boys traveled along the Great Platte across Indian Territory. Some Californians feared attack, but in reality, these people were entrepreneurs...true Americans in a real sense. Potawatomi, Pawnee, Kickapoo, and other tribes who were forced west in the preceding decades, sold supplies to wagon trains, charged tolls at bridges, and ran ferries across rivers and streams. Displaced by invaders in the preceding decades, they once again witnessed thousands of Americans crossing their land. With time, their new homeland would be taken as well. Many Americans called it progress; to the victims, it was nothing short of a crime.

By early August, the group passed by Ft. Kearny and moved on to Ft. Laramie. According to the roadometers affixed to the wagons, the company was now almost 700 miles away from St. Joseph, Missouri. Due to their late start, the Ohio Boys agreed to not rest on the Sabbath. Some of the more religious men felt morally conflicted over this decision. They were still almost 1,100 miles away from the gold-laden gravel of California, and at this pace, they would not reach their destination until well into November. That was too close to tempting fate. Early snow storms in the Rockies or in the Sierra Nevada Mountains could be deadly. Echoes of the ill-fated Donner Party, trapped by November snow in the Sierra Nevadas, resonated with all who approached those barriers in the fall. Only forty-eight of the eighty-seven party members survived, and many of those only because they resorted to eating the flesh of the dead. The Ohio Boys figured God would understand if they traveled on Sundays. Besides, their success not only depended on getting there in one piece, but it also mattered when they arrived. Or, rather, if they arrived before the thousands of other treasure-seekers. It was a race; a race against the seasons; a race against those crossing the continent and arriving by sea; a race to stake a claim.

The race west was evident everywhere. Each day, companies hurried to get underway in the morning, not only to put miles under their feet but also to try to avoid being stuck behind another train and the choking dust they'd generate. Competition became especially tense when approaching passable sections of a river or stream, or when the only feasible way across the land was through a narrow gap. Tempers could flare, fists could fly, and firearms could be drawn. It was no small thing. Each man, team, and company were fighting, mostly in a metaphorical way, to reach their goal in the quickest manner possible. Danny and Stephen had witnessed it firsthand.

Approaching the Deer Creek crossing, the Ohio Boys purchased two sturdily-built rafts for thirty dollars each from a company that had just finished crossing. This was a steep price, but they would recoup the expense by selling them to the next company waiting to cross. But with two rafts, the crossing was slow, but probably safer than removing the wheels from the wagons, caulking the seams, and then floating them across. They found that the best method for them was to unhitch the teams, drive them across the swollen creek, and then ferry the wagons across one at a time. No sense in jeopardizing the whole process by having a team of oxen spook while on the raft, capsizing the vehicle, and losing everything. The whole process went off without a hitch. Danny and Stephen volunteered to be one of the last two teams to cross. Kinney arranged for another company, a much smaller group consisting of four teams, to purchase the rafts.

As the last two teams belonging to the Ohio Boys crossed, two men from the company that purchased the rafts rode with each raft to return to the other side of the creek and begin their crossing process. While Danny and Stephen were harnessing their oxen and reattaching them to their rig, they watched the rafts approach the other bank of the creek. They saw what appeared to be a brewing quarrel between the small company and a small group of men. Danny recognized those men, especially the tall one with the shaved head. It was the Roberts Boys. Luckily, they hadn't seen them since the dustup on the first day in the Ohio Boy's camp. But sure enough, it looked like them.

Roberts heatedly pointed at the returning rafts, and, by his body language, appeared to be intimidating the company members. The situation grew tense as the company leader shook his head and motioned across the creek. Apparently, the Roberts Boys were unwilling to wait their turn or pay the price demanded for the rafts. Either way, words turned to shoves, shoves turned to punches, and a full-out battle was underway. Danny and Stephen held a special dislike for Roberts and his men, and they were eager to get involved. They halted the work of harnessing their teams, and they were now discussing the prospect of swimming across the creek to aid the company. That is until Kinney rode up and admonished the boys that it wasn't their fight and that they had a job to do. He was right, and reluctantly, they finished with their team to venture on with the company.

As the company moved forward, and they walked on, Danny and Stephen saw the rafts land and the four men scrambled up the bank to aid their company. In their haste, they failed to secure the rafts, and it was but just a moment that the craft, first one and then the other, dislodged from the bank and began to float with the current. The combatants, both the company and the Roberts Boys, turned from battling each other to running toward the creek to recover the rafts that were at the mercy of the current. No longer their concern, Danny and Stephen marched on.

***

Perhaps the most difficult portion of the trip west was between South Pass—the Continental Divide—and the Sierra Nevada. Between the points were over fifty miles of desert. The late summer heat baked what passed for soil until it cracked. What little water there was in the wasteland was deadly; unfit to drink because of the alkaline, and further poisoned by the carcasses of dead horses, oxen, and mules. The Ohio Boys, as with many Californians, were acutely aware of the dangers ahead. Throughout the journey, tell-tale signs of problems were listed for all to see. Those who gave up on their quest wrote notes and messages on anything they could—bones, rocks, paper. These were warnings about the expanse of desert and the bad water. Suggestions on which routes were the best, and who took which route. Many chose to take Sublette's and then Hudspeth's Cut-offs. These were trails, some would call them shortcuts, which took a more direct route west than the Oregon Trail. Others, such as the Ohio Boys, thought it wise to detour along the Mormon Trail to Salt Lake City to rest and resupply for two days.

For the Ohio Boys, this was a welcome respite. In Salt Lake City, all the creature comforts that the men had missed were available for a price. Fresh meat, fresh fruit and vegetables, and fresh bread could be had at prices the men didn't consider too high. There were baths and rooms for rent if that was so desired. And there were women. Not women of the night, so-called soiled doves. These were women, which were a sight for eyes that hadn't seen a woman for a couple of months. The movement west to California, at least in the initial phases, was largely a male event. Whole families moved to places like the Oregon Country and the Salt Lake region, but that wasn't the case with California. Families meant settlement and a civilized society. They meant permanence. It was families who "won" the West. American families would eventually join the families of many stripes in California as it was brought into the fold of the Union. That would happen over time. Until then, women and children were somewhat an oddity on the Overland Trail to California. To see them in Salt Lake City, even if just for a couple of days, felt like a special treat.

So, in Salt Lake City they prepared for their big push. The next leg would take them from Salt Lake along Hasting's Cut-off to the Humboldt River, and then across the high desert to where the trail split between the Lassen Cut-off and the Truckee-Carson Routes. From there, they could either choose to take the Carson Trail, following the Carson River, eventually crossing over to the American River, passing by where it all began, Sutter's Fort, and then end their venture as a company at Sacramento City, or they could take the Truckee Trail that led over the rugged Sierra Nevada and its numerous streams, eventually leading to Sacramento City. Many companies and individual travelers chose the Lassen Cut-off, but by the time the Ohio

Boys reached the division in the trail, it was known that the Lassen route was longer. They also heard of the desperation of those taking the Carson Trail—extreme thirst, dying animals, stuck wagons, and abandoned possessions. It wasn't that the Truckee Route was any easier, but it seemed to be the most direct route into California, which is the reason the Ohio Boys chose that trail.

The company bought or traded extra equipment and tools for extra wooden casks and filled them with water, and as many fresh provisions that could be consumed before they spoiled. They also bought extra feed and were able to sell injured oxen and replace those damaged stock with animals that were in better shape. Their two days of rest did much to rejuvenate the members of the company, even if it was just the relief from walking west for two days.

Mostly refreshed, the company continued; the incessant marching, camping, herding, chores, and whatnot performed again and again. By the end of November, they reached the split into California. Light flurries of snow had fallen on them as they neared the Humboldt, causing several members of the team to become fearful of the trudging nature of a loaded-down company. Eight of the men opted to break away from the company, choosing to carry their meager belongings in backpacks they slung over their shoulders. They took as much food and water as Kinney believed was their share, banded together, and moved on at a much quicker pace. This was not the option

Danny and Stephen pursued, opting for the adage that there was safety in numbers.

Safety, however, didn't equate to ease of travel. After leaving the sink of the Humboldt River, the company ran along the edge of the Forty-Mile Desert. Loose, sandy soil, frigid nights, and a lack of water (except that which came with rain and snow) made travel for the company especially difficult. The only naturally-existing water in this desert region was in the form of alkaline hot springs. Heeding the advice left on notes and from merchants in Salt Lake City, the Ohio Boys purchased extra kegs for water. But many emigrants drank from the putrid water, causing severe stomach cramps and extreme cases of loose bowels. That was a situation that the Ohio Boys were lucky enough to avoid. However, it was just one less difficult of many that they faced.

Among the highest of peaks in the distance snow was an ominous reminder that it was now even closer to winter than they wanted it to be. But they still moved forward, determined to beat their way into California...snow or no snow. By the time that the company had reached the Truckee River, several of the units lost oxen. Overworked and undernourished, stock refused to walk anymore, or dropped dead in their tracks. This forced the men to con-solidate—abandon wagons, take stock of their supplies, weed out truly unnecessary supplies and objects, and com-bine teams. The unit that Danny and Stephen were in lost one of their teams, reducing the total number of wagons in their unit to three. Overall, the Ohio Boys lost a total of six teams. The dead and dying animals, combined with broken-down buckboards and discarded items, symbolized the struggle every emigrant experienced. Luckily, Stephen's wagon was still in one piece, and they still had three of their oxen, a fact that allowed them to potentially sell their investment in California to recoup expenses and outfit for the gold fields. As long as they made it relatively intact.

Choosing the Truckee Trail was its own special type of Hell. The Truckee River flowed fast and deep for a good portion of the year. Since they were moving through the region in late Fall, the water was also brisk. Unfortunately for the company, the trail didn't parallel the river through the Sierras. The trail crossed the Truckee River twenty-seven times! Each crossing imperiled the company. Oxen could lose their footing, wagons or gear could be swept away, and equipment could break. That's not to mention the fact that the men were subjected time and again to the water, chilling them to the bone, in addition to threatening their wellbeing if rushing water knocked them off their feet, soaking them to the bone at best, drowning them or hastening a case of hypothermia at its worst.

Regardless of the river crossings, the company also had to ascend and descend ridges and gorges, which was never an easy feat. And then there were the boulders and rock fields that had to be traversed. Complicating all of this was making their way through all of these obstacles, at times with snow on the ground in some places, blowing wind, and freezing rain. It made for a miserable existence and required extra exertion. Muscles ached and burned; none of the food they had was satisfying; every person grumbled about the circumstances; even the stock seemed to complain with their moans and groans, day and night. Betsy and Penny stressed near death, and the hens only avoided freezing to death because Danny packed extra straw into their crate, gave them extra feed, and placed them near the fire at night. They survived the Truckee Trail but had refused to produce eggs since the Big Sink. The hardship tended to mask the beauty around them—high mountain lakes; towering pines, cedars, and firs; massive domes of granite; and the stars at night.

But as they crested the Sierra Nevada, they began to finally feel as though their struggle to get to California was nearing an end. Passing through Bear Valley, Mule Springs, Steep Hollow Creek, Cedar Ravine, and Greenhorn Creek the trail spilled out into the Sacramento Valley. The gently rolling hills, punctuated by oak trees and good grass, were a welcome sight to the Ohio Boys, let alone any of the emigrants, who were now, metaphorically and physically, Californians.

Chapter 6
A Melting Pot

———— •••◆••• ————

From July to December 1849, the Ohio Boys marched 1,800 miles across the continent. They worked together, ate together, camped together, struggled together. When ill, they aided each other. They laughed and cried; cursed their situation and dreamt of what could be. And now? Now they had reached California and were set to go their separate ways to seek their fortunes, whatever they may be.

Jim Kinney and the other officers brought them together, and it was now their duty to muster all of the men out of the company. Supplies owned by the company, such as food and tools, were divvied up. Men made their rounds, shaking hands and patting each other on the back. Many of the men promised to try to keep in touch with each other. Some men continued their partnership, forming a mining company. Recognizing that many hands made quick work this seemed a practical step to take. Danny and Stephen joined with Albert and Jeremiah Swanson to form the Two Hens Mining Company, a homage to those two ragged hens that Danny hauled from Missouri. Collectively, they had a wagon, two oxen—two were sold for supplies—picks and shovels, two tents, a small metal stove, cooking utensils, bedding, clothing, and the basic materials they figured they'd need to stake a claim.

Arriving at the beginning of December, however, wasn't an optimal situation. Snow was now falling heavily in the mountains, the ground grew hard and cold, and the rivers and streams bearing gravel, crevices, and sand that sheltered gold ran clear, but near freezing. The creeks, streams, and rivers had lower flows, allowing for easier access to gravel and sandbars, but that was all weighed against that frigid water.

Mining would prove to the thousands of prospectors to be some of the most difficult work they had ever done. Marching across the continent was, to say the least, a most challenging proposition. But mining was miserable in its own way. It didn't matter the season, men dug dirt, hauled dirt, panned dirt, sifted dirt, and washed dirt. They dammed waterways, diverted waterways, and constructed sloughs to bring water long distances where it was needed. If a claim didn't produce, miners sought a new claim, chasing new strikes, all the while believing that it was soon to be their time. These tasks were repeatedly performed.

Some men became wealthy from their work, but most men barely covered their expenses. Most of the men who struck it rich were those who mined the miners—providing the goods and services, at grossly inflated prices, to those who sought their fortunes in the form of gold. Of course, the amount of money one could charge essentially depended on where goods were bought, as well as when the items were purchased. Early in the Gold Rush, when supplies were scarce and demand was high, premium prices could be levied. As time went on, when more supplies flooded into California and merchants became more numerous and closer in proximity to the mining camps, prices declined. Take for example the price charged for a pickaxe. In the mining camps in 1848, an entrepreneur could charge as much as fifty dollars for a single pickaxe. An outfitter in Sacramento City might charge as much as twenty-five dollars for each pickaxe in that same year. However, two years later in 1850, merchants might offer two pickaxes for $10.50. Either way, the prices were inflated and enterprising individuals with forethought could make a killing supplying miners.

The four men of the Two Hens Mining Company decided to rest for a few days before they headed into the field. Their sorry state after crossing into California almost too late in the season required a short rejuvenation. This allowed for them to wash and mend clothing, shave and bathe, refit for mining, and explore Sacramento City.

Born in 1848 around the docks built at the convergence of the American and Sacramento Rivers by John Sutter and his son, John Sutter, Jr., Sacramento City became a major staging area for hopeful miners heading to the western slopes of the Sierra Nevada Mountains. In its early existence, the city was amazingly absent of saloons, gambling houses, and brothels. But human nature prevailed, and by the time the Ohio Boys arrived, there were plenty of these establishments scattered throughout the 800 buildings, tents, and false-fronted structures. The rivers were a double-edged sword for the city. The wharf that was constructed enabled extensive trade, which was the lifeblood of the city. Boats of all shapes and sizes brought goods from the San Francisco Bay. But the rivers also brought destruction. The original city was built on a floodplain. All it took was for the Sacramento or American Rivers, or both, as in 1850, to crest their banks and flood the settlement. After several massive floods, the city's sidewalks and buildings were raised well above the floodplain, and a series of dykes and levees were constructed to protect against rising water.

In the afternoon of their second full day in Sacramento City, as Stephen, Albert, and Jeremiah were out securing needed supplies, Danny stayed with their gear. He spent time feeding his hens and examining their condition. They were still in alive, which was a good thing, but they were still stressed. Danny constructed a makeshift yard for the hens to run around in, giving them some much-needed time out of their crate.

Danny was daydreaming, tossing small amounts of feed to the hens when he heard a nasally, high-pitched voice addressing him.

"Them there's some sorry-looking birds."

Snapping out of his lazy daze, Danny looked at the man. He was bearded, about five and a half feet tall, with a weathered look about his face, hands, and clothes. Everything about the man gave Danny the perception that he'd been around and had experience. That, or he had some of the worst hygiene and a total lack of social conscience.

"But they ain't dead, which is a good thing," the man said as a matter of fact. "Where abouts you from?"

Danny informed the man that he and his friend were from Missouri, and the other two men in their mining crew were from Ohio.

"You musta taken the overland route, then. You're a bit late to the diggings, greenhorn! No cabin...icy water...frozen ground. Ya picked a Hell of a time to get started!"

Taken aback by the man's straightforward temperament, Danny tried to take in what he was saying without feeling offended.

"So, old-timer...you're saying that I should just give up? Head back home?"

"Don't get your feathers all ruffled there, young man. I ain't saying that at all. Ya just arrived a bit late," the man said in a tone that was a little less abrasive.

"And you ain't the only one...look around." The man motioned to the numerous people going about their business.

"It's just the nature of this beast. Once word of Marshall's find got out...well...there's people from all over this damn world that want a piece of the action. There's the Americans already here and those who came down from the Oregon Country...the Sonorans who came up from Mexico. And your Chileans and those from Peru. Sandwich Island peoples. O' course them Indians was already here. Frenchies and Brits...the Celestials..."

"Celestials?" Danny inquired.

"The Chinamen," the man clarified. "Seems like God ordered folks from all around to come here."

And the man was correct. When gold was discovered, people from all around the world sought to reach California, quickly increasing the population of the soon-to-be state. It's estimated that in 1848, the non-Indian population in California was around 10,000 people. Within two years, though, the population ballooned to over 200,000. The non-native population was added to by folks from all around, near and far. From the states and territories, Mexico, South America, Canada, Europe, the Pacific Islands, and Asia. They were a spectrum of the races: whites, blacks, Asians. In regards to the amount of diversity, California was perhaps the most "American" place possessed by the United States.

If being American meant subjugating Indians, Californians embraced their American heritage with vigor. Indians faced the gamut of treatment from emigrants. Many were exploited as cheap labor and worked in gangs to move dirt and water. Or they were hunted down like animals, killed, or driven from the land. But it wasn't just the Americans that perpetrated this treatment. In many ways, it was a continuation of policies enacted in Alta California, first by the Spanish and then by Mexicans.

"Young man. Mind if ol' Cooper gives ya a bit of advice?"

Eager for success, and in acknowledgment of the man's experience, Danny relayed that he'd appreciate it.

"First thing to do when ya stake your claim is to post a notice and leave a shovel or pick on the site. It's best to even dig a little hole...disturb the earth. Put up some markers or build a cairn of rocks. But don't waste too much time on that. Ya need to build a cabin and get together enough wood to keep you warm. There'll be time for diggin'...hell, you'll soon be sick of diggin'. Find you a place near water...that's where you'll be working."

"If ya have any extra money, buy yourself some goods that ya can sell in the camps...flour...boots...bacon. You're bound to make more money selling supplies this winter than by pulling any gold out of that ground."

"And while you be here in town, by God, avoid any and all of those dens of sin. Those merchants of booze and of the flesh are more than willin' to rob ya blind. Same thing goes for those gamblin' houses. They ain't built on winners!"

These words were the truth. Men flocked from the mining camps to drink away their troubles. If their misery couldn't be alleviated through the bottom of a bottle, then they could at least enjoy the company of others who shared their circumstances. Misery loves company. Many men who were disappointed in their lack of wealth from their claims sought to strike it rich at Faro, poker, or any number of other games of chance and supposed skill. This avenue to prosperity rarely worked out in the favor of the patron. The house typically had the advantage in fair games, and most certainly in games that were rigged. And the flesh trade? Men, lacking female companionship, visited the dance houses for a fandango, or the brothels for the rented touch of the opposite sex. They got what they paid for but at the cost of disease and guilt. And that's not to mention the impact on the women who were subjected to violence and disease. The high rates of alcoholism and drug use, as well as elevated rates of suicide, were rampant among the "fallen women."

"Be industrious, young man. Use what's in your head, and take an opportunity when you can," the man said as he picked up his pack from the ground, slinging it over his shoulder.

"Thanks, old-timer," Danny stated as the man began to walk on. "Good luck to ya!"

The man laughed and waved off the gesture. "Luck? I'm off to get me a bath, a bottle, a game of Faro, and some lovin'. And not necessarily in that order!" He sounded like a lunatic as he laughed and laughed, walking away like a man on a mission.

Danny figured that what the man had to say was based on experience. It's good to learn from your mistakes. But it's better to learn from the mistakes of others. Perhaps the man was the best teacher in California.

***

With the return of his partners, Danny went on an errand of his own. If what old man Cooper said was true, then maybe there was some money to be made off supplies. Danny went to the nearest merchant, a man he learned was Samuel Brannan, a Mormon emigrant and successful businessman. There was a wide variety of goods to be had at the store, and with a little over thirty dollars, Danny purchased a selection of goods he believed would be in demand—three India-rubber backed canvas tarps, ten pounds of flour, two gallons of molasses, and another laying hen he'd call Tilly. Brannan was getting the better end of the deal, even if he gave Danny a discount on the hen, but that's the way business goes. Danny was taking a risk. Worst case scenario, he and his partners would use the supplies.

Having traveled the Truckee Trail, the most logical place for the newly-formed mining company to stake a claim was along the North Fork of the American River. So, onward they went, out of the valley, into the foothills, and up along the American River. They passed through an assortment of mining camps, some large, others rather small. It was easy to tell which camps were more success-ful by the population of the camp, their equipment, and the spirit of the men working there. Nothing disguises a wretched existence like the victory of success; men will push themselves through incredible circumstances if they believe, and know, that the effort is worth the trouble. And the other camps? The struggle and hardship could be seen on the faces of the men—sunken and glazed-over eyes, the disheveled clothing, the sullen look on their faces, and the negativity and tension that reverberated from their very existence. Danny and his partners hoped they could avoid that sad situation.

After four days of following the American River looking for a location to stake a claim, and ultimately pushing far-ther up the North Fork due to the number of miners, the boys found a likely spot near the convergence of Shirttail

Creek and the American River. It was here that each member of the company staked a claim, twelve feet by twelve feet, on a gravel and sand bar in the creek, on two sides of the creek, and in a dry gully that ran down to the creek. The four corners of each claim were hastily, but clearly, marked with wooden poles that were four feet high. Attached to a pole on each claim was a note with the name of the owner. Even though the claims were technically owned by the paper-holder, each member of the group affirmed that they would work the claims in common for mutual benefit. Each man believed in their heart that they could trust their brothers in mining. They crossed the continent together; they would mine and hopefully prosper together.

Although they were eager to begin their search for gold, they did realize that a simple home was necessary. The rain and snow, as well as the heat of the summer, would be unbearable without a proper cabin. But until that could be built, they erected their tents and made a temporary home. Danny created a small yard for Penny, Betsy, and Tilly using sticks and branches as a fence to prevent them from wandering off, but allow them more room to forage and stretch their legs. He also modified their crate to work as a small hen house. It was crude and cramped, but it would work until he had time to build a larger one.

They also tried their hand at panning for gold, although their lack of knowledge was apparent. But try, they did. They'd dig a shovelful of dirt, place it in the pan, and begin the washing process. Squatting ankle-deep in the creek, they swished water around in the pan, washing away the dirt and pebbles. It was a slow and delicate process. The trick was to allow the water and gravity to separate the heavier gold from the lighter materials, such as sand and dirt. If you worked the pan with too much vigor, there was the very real possibility that gold would be lost and dumped back into the creek. The four men slowly picked up on the process through trial and error, but mostly error. But it'd be dreams of what could be that kept their enthusiasm at a premium.

On a cold, misty morning in late December, Danny and Stephen were working on the group's cabin. They'd already felled several pine trees, limbed them, cut them into eighteen-foot sections, and used their oxen to drag them down from a nearby ridge. The bottom three layers of the cabin were nicely shaping up. A base of flat rocks, numerous along the creek, kept the bottom logs off the ground to prevent rot. Where the corners came together, notches were cut into the logs to create a tight, secure fit, and they planned their structure to have one door and one window. It was a typical log cabin, the type built in America for generations. It was a simple; constructed more to protect the men from the elements, and less for its looks. In time, the chinking of clay, grass, and pine needles would fill the cracks between the logs to better insulate the cabin and attempt to keep unwanted creatures out.

To secure the entrance, a rough wooden door with leather hinges would be added, and a wooden plank would cover the window during the winter, but removed during the warmer months to allow for better ventilation. The men also planned to build a stone fireplace. To top off the cabin, trusses, purlins, and a ridge pole would be laid. Eventually, they would construct a proper roof with shingles, but until that time, they would use two of their rubber-backed tarps as a transitory roof.

The sounds of axes created muffled echoes as Stephen and Danny worked on two logs, chopping a pair of matching notches. Foggy plumes of their breath could be seen in the cold.

"I'm not sure what I'd rather be doing," Stephen managed between axe swings and breaths, "working the dirt in that frigid creek, or building this cabin."

"At least we're keeping warm," Danny responded between his labored breathing and swings.

"Good point, but I ain't come here to build a cabin."

Stephen was speaking the truth that all miners dealt with. Everyday tasks that had to be done were distractions; chores that prevented the men from doing what they came here to do. Whether it was cutting firewood, cooking meals, or building shelters, it had to be done. Danny and Stephen's gnawing desire to pan for gold would have to wait.

They rolled the logs together to check the fit of the notches.

"Not bad," Danny relayed as they assessed their work. "We could always go into the cabin-building business...just think, who wants to waste their time doing all of this work? We could make a fortune!"

Danny was half-kidding, realizing that there was more than one way to make a living.

Stephen shook his head at that idea. "Naw, I coulda stayed at home and been a laborer. No, thank you!"

Time passed as they fit another layer of the cabin. Maybe Stephen was right, Danny thought. But Danny was keeping an open mind. One way or another he was determined to make his way.

From down on the creek, Jeremiah called to his partners. There was excitement in his voice, bordering on panic.

"Boys! Come down here! Ya have to see this!" Jeremiah shouted to Albert, Stephen, and Danny. Looking at each other, Stephen and Danny dropped their tools and ran down the trail to one of the claims. Albert put his pan down and trudged through the water over to Jeremiah.

"Look at that! Just look at that!" Jeremiah practically screamed in the faces of his partners, pointing at three little specks of gold. About the size of sesame seeds, the yellowish objects were exactly what the men needed to feed their hunger. It would intensify their fever for gold; an obsession was born.

Jeremiah continued, "This was my second pan from that sand bar. I need...I need something to put it in!"

"I'll get a jar," Jeremiah's brother, Albert, volunteered as he ran back up the trail to his tent.

"I'll be damned," Stephen said with wonder. He carefully picked up one of the specks and rolled it between his fingers. "I'll be damned! This is it, boys! This is what we came for!"

Stephen placed the little pebble of gold back in the pan and ran to get his tools. Danny did the same. In no time at all, all four partners were down in the water working the earth. That creek water wasn't as cold as it was before they found gold. Excitement has a way of tempering the senses. They were more than willing to test their stamina now that it was worth the effort.

From dawn until dusk, at least two of the men were working at any given time on their claims. Just to break even, they needed to find one ounce of gold a day, valued at about sixteen dollars. But their claim was proving to be better than average. Over the next week, the placer mine produced between two and nine ounces a day, and they accumulated almost twenty-two ounces of gold, enough to almost cover half of what it cost the men to reach California. They stored their gold nuggets and dust in that jar, watching the empty space slowly disappear. Their mood became jovial. Their hopes and aspirations were becoming their reality. However, the work wasn't any easier, it was just more pleasurable because of their success.

And that success trickled into other avenues, as well. The cabin, for what it was, was completed in three weeks. It provided a mostly dry space, and with a fire in the hearth, was warm and cozy in the evenings. Danny's hens were altogether producing at least two eggs a day. With any luck, Danny planned to purchase a couple more hens, and maybe a rooster, the next time he was in Sacramento City. The Two Hens Mining Company, now a misnomer, was by all accounts, heading for prosperity.

***

For three weeks the weather held. It was cold, especially in the mornings and at night, but the daytime was tolerable. Snow came to the higher elevations, but down lower where they were, they experienced rain; light at first, and then a heavy downpour. Prospectors were already partially soaked from standing in the rushing water, so a light rain wasn't much of a deterrent. A heavy rainstorm, however, was an entirely different story. Creeks, streams, and rivers become swollen and dangerous. The speed of the water, and the amount of floating debris, created a situation where working in the water was borderline negligence. On days like these, most men found shelter inside and did chores or tried to relax. For others, especially those newcomers, inclement weather expounded their despair. But somebody's need can also become another person's opportunity, especially if an individual recognizes the situation and is willing to take a chance based on their hunch. That person was Danny. Based on Cooper's advice, he'd purchased the tarps, flour, and molasses. With the rain, men who haven't built log cabins would likely experience hardship; the rain soaking men and materials. Surely, Danny would be able to sell the tarps he purchased.

Danny told his partners what he planned, and since it was raining and the amount of prospecting that'd be done was little to none, they were receptive. They understood that Danny, like them, was trying to plan for his future. Danny didn't find it difficult to convince his partners to allow him to venture out for a day or two, especially when he sweetened the deal by cutting them in on a small portion of the profits. A man becomes more agreeable to a situation when they have something to gain. Danny spent his own money on the supplies, and he'd retain the majority of the profit, but the partnership would also benefit without putting forth the risk or effort.

Danny and Albert hitched the oxen to the wagon and loaded the rubber-backed tarps, four eggs, and seven skinny logs measuring approximately ten feet each. Not knowing how long they'd be gone, they also packed a tent, some rations, and Danny's shotgun. Even though Albert had no obligation to go with Danny, he volunteered, largely because he was bored and wanted to see more than the four walls of their cabin.

Figuring that the most likely candidates for his goods were those miners who recently arrived and were the farthest away from Sacramento City, they chose to take the team up the American River. Within a quarter of a mile from their claim, Danny and Albert passed through other camps. Some were well-established, with proper, if not rustic, cabins. At each camp, the two stopped to assess the situation, gossip, and generally be neighborly. The first few camps did not need the logs or the tarps, but the eggs were in high demand. Danny was able to sell his eggs for three dollars worth of gold. Additionally, the men in the camp told Danny that they'd buy all of the eggs he brought them. This was a nice prospect for Danny, and with some planning, he could provide a steady source of income for himself and his partners.

Farther up the river Danny and Albert found another camp that was not as prepared, having arrived at the diggings no more than a day before. They looked like soaked rats. With one tent barely standing and the rest of their gear in disarray, they were off to a rough start.

"Howdy friends," Danny announced as he rolled toward their camp, "mind if we enter?"

There was a welcome break in the rain, allowing for their conversation to be held at the wagon. Two men and a woman temporarily stopped what they were doing. A man in his early thirties seemed to be the leader or spokesperson for the camp.

"Not at all...please, come in," the man warmly answered. "Name's Carl Banks...that there's my wife Julia, and my brother David. I'd offer you some coffee, but our situation is a bit...well...you can see, we're just trying to figure things out."

Carl Banks and his family arrived in California a short time ago, just after Danny and the Ohio Boys. Their journey, though, was quite different from those jumping off from Missouri. They were from New England. Massachusetts to be exact. Carl was a teacher and his brother worked as a fisherman. Just like thousands of other Americans, they were inspired to come to California to seek their fortunes. But they chose to come by sea; from the states, down the east coast of South America, around the Horn, up the west coast of South and North America, and then into San Francisco Bay. The 15,000-mile trip was terrifying; the angry seas produced monster swells that threatened to pound ships in the Southern Atlantic. The air and water, capable of icing up the rigging, rails, and deck, added to the trials that the seasick passengers experienced. That route was relatively quick, though. The ship the Banks family was on made the journey in five months.

Arriving at San Francisco Bay, their eyes couldn't believe what they saw—there were seemingly hundreds of ships anchored and abandoned. A flotilla that was unable to ply the waters due to a lack of crews. Once word of the gold strike reached the wharves and the rest of the world, crew members looked for their first opportunity to jump ship. It was said that a person could practically walk across the Bay by hopping the short distance from deck to deck. And San Francisco...the sleepy little town of 800 people in 1848 had grown to over 25,000 by the end of 1850.

Disembarked, they purchased the gear they were told they needed, but they were woefully unprepared and undersupplied. Danny and Albert took a look at their tent and advised them to add some support beams to better give shape to the canvas and prevent rainfall from gathering in the sagging pockets.

Seeing an opportunity to help the Banks family, and make some extra funds, Danny made his pitch.

"Carl, we just happen to have some supplies you and your family could use," Danny delicately introduced the proposition. "Heck, we can even give you a hand fitting out your tent."

Hesitant, largely due to pride, Carl hemmed and hawed at the offer. "I don't know, boys. I'm sure my brother and I will be just fine."

"Just think, Carl...the sooner you are set, the sooner you can work your claim," Danny countered. "Out here, time truly is money. Without a secure camp, you'll just waste time...over and over...making repairs. I already have some poles that can be cut to size and fit as ridge poles, and two India tarps that will help keep the rain from seeping through your tent. Me, Albert, and our other partners have already done this...we know how to do it right the first time."

Carl thought this over. It was a convincing argument, based on need and logic. But he knew it wouldn't be free.

"That might make sense," Carl assented, "but everything has a cost." He looked, first at Albert and then at Danny, asking, "What's your cost?"

Danny was counting on Carl being used to the inflated prices of the West. Tallying his expenses and what he believed would be a fair price, Danny confidently stated, "We can do it all for thirty-five dollars."

"Thirty-five dollars? Well...that's a bit steep," Carl plainly stated. He did expect an inflated price, although he wasn't above negotiating. "Give me a moment to talk this over with my wife and brother."

Carl walked back to his family and whispered in conference with his people. He didn't take too long, nodding in agreement with his brother and wife, and then walked back to the boys.

"Gentlemen, I know you have something we could use...and I know you're aware of that fact. Would you take thirty dollars...and, say...a pound of potatoes, a pound of onions, and a pound of sugar?"

Danny had already made up his mind, but he included Albert in the decision-making process since his labor was also needed.

"Carl, you've got yourself a deal," Danny stated after Albert agreed with the price.

The two men immediately got to work, measuring, cutting, notching, and lashing the poles together in a frame, essentially constructing a tent cabin. They placed the India tarps on top of the tent, overlapping the material to prevent water from running under the seams, and then secured the corners. Thinking to keep his customers happy, Danny illustrated to Carl and his brother how to adjust the India tarps when they became askew. All of this took only about two hours.

With the task complete and pleased with the outcome, both parties thanked each other. Before leaving, Danny told Carl that his camp could be found on Shirttail Creek near the American River and that when they found some gold, and if they wanted a structure that was a bit more comfortable, then maybe they could come to an agreement on the cost of lumber and labor. Carl wouldn't commit, stating that it's always an option.

Danny and Albert both mounted the buckboard and headed back home. It was a successful business venture. With three dollars in gold, thirty dollars in U.S. currency, and a pound each of sugar, potatoes, and onions Danny was coming out ahead. He decided to add one dollar in gold to the jar, and one dollar in currency toward the partnership. He also gave Albert two dollars in currency and secured an agreement from him that anytime he needed his help, he'd be there.

They arrived home in the evening, unhitched the team, and tended to their needs. Triumphantly, Danny and Albert told their partners about their day, showed them the earnings, and revealed the items that were bartered for their labor. The rain had started again, but it didn't matter to them at that moment. Danny fried up some bacon, made some fritters out of flour, water, and eggs to bake in a Dutch oven, and then fried some potatoes and onions in the bacon grease. It was simple food, but to them, they were eating like kings.

***

Throughout January and February of 1850, the partners continued their efforts. Their methods, however, had changed a bit. The pick and shovel were still essential for the movement of dirt, and the pan was still used to process test samples and more precisely separate gold dust from sand. But necessity was the mother of invention. When visiting other camps, the partners picked up new ideas on how to process the dirt and reclaim the gold. The use of a simple rocker box or rocker cradle increased the speed at which gravel and dirt were washed. Using a rocker doubled the amount of material that a single man with a pan could process. A shovelful of earth was placed in the top opening of the box. Water was ladled over the material as the box was carefully rocked back and forth like a baby cradle. Larger items, such as gravel, were retained on a top grate, and smaller particles, such as sand and gold, fell through to make their way across a series of wooden riffles. In theory, and typically in practice, the heavier gold was trapped behind the riffles. Many boxes also had a carpet-like material, called miner's moss, that lined the bottom of the box to trap fine gold. When the riffles and moss were cleaned out, the materials were sorted using a pan and a smooth hand. The boys constructed a rocker and found a great deal of success in its ease of use.

More effective was the construction and use of a sluice box. This implement took a bit more work, but could process even more material than the rocker. Gravel and dirt were shoveled into a receiving box. Running water, diverted from the creek through a ditch or flume, constantly washed over the material and pushed it down a trough-like box that was at least six feet long. Just like the rocker, riffles and moss were used to collect the gold. Some companies, larger and more organized than the Two Hens, built what was called Long Toms. These were like regular sluice boxes but with multiple troughs running longer distances. Of course, these contraptions required a larger number of workers.

Regardless of the design, twice a day the riffles and moss were cleaned, and materials caught by the riffles were processed using a pan. Unlike the rocker, which could be operated by two people, the sluice box the Two Hens built required at least three people to operate, although the attention of all four men maximized its efficiency. When the partners worked along the creek they utilized the sluice box, otherwise they hauled buckets of water to use with their rocker.

Chapter 7
New Directions

———◆◆◆◆◆———

B y the end of February, the boys were ready to take their gold down to Sacramento City to exchange for supplies and currency. With two and a half months of sporadic work, the company pulled 198 ounces of gold dust and nuggets from the ground. Danny had also managed to sell two dozen eggs and ten pounds of flour for thirty-seven dollars in gold. Additionally, Danny gathered all the letters to be mailed from surrounding camps and offered to deliver them to post in Sacramento for fifty cents in gold each, accounting for an additional six dollars in gold. He had plans to expand his business enterprise. Altogether, he had forty-five dollars in gold and twenty-seven dollars in silver dollars, more than enough to purchase another hen and a rooster.

Realizing that better weather was just around the corner and that every day brought more single men into the surrounding country, Danny was gambling on another business prospect. He had visited the Banks' camp and found that they weren't doing as well as they hoped. They found some gold, but the pickings were slim. Maybe it was the weather. Perhaps they were just in the wrong location. But their economic potential was, in Danny's estimation, untapped. Julia Banks was a wonderful cook. Once mining season roared back to life with better weather, hungry men possessing gold will be more than willing to part with some of their earnings for a home-cooked meal. Added to that was the fact that Julia was the only woman within 15 to 20 miles. That alone may draw men to the Banks' kitchen. If they couldn't have a wife, they could at least enjoy her presence during a meal. With some compromise, Danny secured a partnership with Julia Banks. Her husband and brother-in-law would continue to prospect, but she would be the sole proprietor of her kitchen. Danny would purchase the supplies and keep her well-stocked in exchange for sixty percent of the profits. It was a mutually beneficial deal...as long as customers showed up.

Not willing to leave their claims unattended, Jeremiah volunteered to stay behind. For him, it wasn't a huge sacrifice. Since he was the most skilled at finding pay dirt and extracting the gold, he'd rather work the claims anyway.

As partners, they continued to have faith and trust in one another. Although not rare, growing prosperity can cause division and jealousy. Is everyone working just as hard? Did one member feel that they deserved a larger portion of gold because they initially located the strike? Was a member squirreling away gold...hiding it from their partners? Many a quarrel resulted in the injury or death of men who once treated each other as brothers. The members of the Two Hens Mining Company weren't like that, though. Even with Danny pursuing other avenues, his fellow members of the partnership didn't wish to push him out. Danny did a fair share of the work, helped around the camp, and dipped into his supplies for camp use. Besides, Danny made his friends aware that he'd make sure that ten percent of his share of the profits from his arrangement with Julia Banks went to the Company. Danny's success was their profit. That was nothing to turn your back on.

With the oxen hitched to the wagon that Danny and Albert rode, and Stephen accompanying them on his horse, the happy crew took the two-day ride into Sacramento. As they passed near camps along the way, Danny inquired if anyone wanted to send a post and how much he'd charge. He wound up stowing away additional mail that earned him eight dollars more in gold.

They stopped each evening near camps, setting up their tent in a feeble attempt to ward off the cold. More often than not, they were invited into the neighboring camp to enjoy their fire and a drink. None of the Two Hens group had spent much time drinking, and having all of their gold in their possession, they imbibed with caution, more out of politeness than the enjoyment of its taste. To have their hard work stolen while in a drunken stupor could have irreversible consequences.

Riding into Sacramento, the men found it difficult to recognize the town they had left three months earlier for two reasons. First, was the chaotic state of the town bordering the Sacramento and American Rivers. By the beginning of January 1850, over seventeen inches of rain fell within two months, more rain than the region typically receives all winter. Both rivers flooded over their banks, spilling a mixture of water, mud, and debris down the town's streets. It was devastating, ruining buildings, washing away goods, and generally causing panic. The waters didn't recede until almost mid-January. Still, the impact of the flood could be seen at the end of February. Erosion was present along the banks, mud was still in portions of the streets, and water damage on the buildings was still present. Where buildings had been swept away or damaged beyond repair, there were empty lots. Luckily, the carcasses of mules, horses, and other animals that couldn't escape the flood waters had all been collected and removed far from town. And what would prove to be beneficial for the town was a system of levees and dykes that men were already constructing. There was also talk of physically raising the buildings and sidewalks.

Second, was the sheer mass of people that, like the rivers, flooded into the town. Sacramento was a busy place in December, but even more so now. Discouraged by the weather or bad luck, many men retreated from the camps to the town. Many more arrived from the Overland Trail and via San Francisco, only to be delayed by the massive amount of rain that fell. So, there was a mixture of people full of anticipation and dreams, and those who experienced limited success and outright failure, pessimistic and bitter to the core. It was a volatile concoction, ripe and eager to find scapegoats. The easiest target for these men to focus on were those who looked nothing like themselves.

Gam Saan, "Gold Mountain" in Cantonese, was the name often used by the Chinese from Toisan in Guangdong to refer specifically to San Francisco, and more generally to California itself. Economically depressed, famine-stricken, and torn by warfare, men from this region in China, like hopeful prospectors from all over the world, jumped at the chance to seek economic security by going to Gold Mountain. Between 1849 and 1853 approximately 24,000 young men arrived from China. Over 20,000 Chinese gold-seekers arrived in 1852 alone. Culturally and physically different, these immigrants tended to live apart from other sectors of the population in California. Seen as an unwillingness to assimilate, this was a survival technique. Humans tend to gravitate toward what is familiar; a veritable comfort zone. Speaking very little English and coming from an area of the world that was culturally and religiously different than the United States,

Chinese immigrants lived and worked together in cohesive communities.

At first, these immigrants were seen as fellow men in search of opportunity. Working as laborers, providing services in the restaurant, hotel, and laundry industries, and miners, whites tolerated their presence and even appreciated the services that were provided at reasonable rates. But as the Gold Rush progressed, and as competition increased for the easy placer gold, animosity mounted. White miners routinely abandoned productive mines to chase new strikes. Chinese miners happily worked these abandoned claims and even the tailings of mines that had seemingly played out. Through their perseverance and cooperation with each other, Chinese miners experienced success, earning more money mining than they could in their native land.

But when adversity came to the mines and men began to find prospecting more difficult and less profitable, they looked for answers. To them, foreigners were the obvious problem. It was the Chinese (as well as Chileans, Peruvians, and Sonorans) who were taking what rightfully belonged to Americans—white Americans. Discounting inclement weather, bad luck, gambling and drinking, inflated prices, or the general increase in the competition for gold from the growing influx of miners from the States, the cause of their decreasing success and mounting distress were these foreigners. When the occasion arose, white miners intimidated foreign miners, pushing them off their claims. When that didn't work, many resulted in physical assault to convince outsiders to move on. Government officials even tried to make work for foreign miners more economically difficult by implementing a Foreign Miner's Tax in 1850 that required miners not eligible for citizenship to pay a twenty-dollar-a-month fee for the privilege to search for gold. The tax was revised to three dollars a month in 1852, but it was still based more on the animosity towards foreigners in the mines, and less on the desire to generate revenue for the State.

Stephen, Danny, and Albert planned to stay no more than one day in Sacramento. There was too much to do at camp, and Danny was eager to deliver supplies to Julia Banks. The sooner that was done, the sooner their partnership would benefit. One positive aspect of more people arriving in California was the increase of goods that were also shipped into the region. More goods meant lower prices. Granted, prices were still inflated, but the purchasing power of consumers increased because of changing circumstances.

In all, Danny purchased fifty pounds of flour, eighteen pounds of salt pork, twenty pounds of salt beef, two gallons of molasses, and twenty pounds each of sugar, potatoes, onions, and coffee. He spent forty-two dollars of his gold for the supplies, all in the hope that the profits produced would be greater many times over. Having eleven dollars in gold left over, Danny added thirteen dollars in silver coins to purchase two more hens and a rooster. He was ambitious, and each of his business decisions was based on intuition but well-calculated. A similar amount of supplies were also acquired by the partners in the Two Hens Company.

The next order of business was transforming their gold dust and nuggets into currency. There were several ways this could be done. Some businessmen who operated as bankers bought gold and issued banknotes or paper currency that were only accepted locally. So, converted wealth was seemingly trapped within the region that recognized the banking entity. Other enterprising individuals bought gold and minted it into coins. The danger with this option was selling valuable gold in exchange for coins that were of lesser quality and were not recognized as official coinage by the United States government. The last option available was to sell their gold for the United States-minted gold and silver coins. This was perhaps the safest option, as long as they were available. Ultimately, they were able to exchange their gold for $3,128 in a combination of twenty-dollar gold pieces, silver dollars, and banknotes. The difficulty in transferring gold into money became easier in 1854 when the United States government established a mint in San Francisco to produce gold coins.

The last thing to do before they began their trip back was to stop by one of the agents to send the letters collected back to the States; to mothers and fathers, siblings and other relatives, wives and girlfriends, and friends. In addition to the letters gathered from the camps, each of the members of the Two Hens Company wrote a letter home, confirming to their loved ones that they were well and on the path toward prosperity. They also informed them where letters could be sent.

As Danny walked to the agent's office, he noticed a small crowd gathered nearby. They were difficult to miss. Loud and boisterous, more than likely full of whiskey, the men were taunting a small group of Chinese men.

"Just look at them...those Chinee heathen," one man said with disgust as he poked in their direction with a stick.

"It's a bunch a coolie girls...pigtails an all!" Another man shouted and the crowd roared into laughter.

Danny pitied the Chinese men, believing that they had a right to be there, just as they did. But it wasn't his fight. To stop the hatred he'd have to fight all of the men in the crowd, and then move on to potentially a larger portion of the white population in California. Feeling somewhat ashamed, he went about his business.

He met with the agent and made arrangements to send the letters on through San Francisco and their destinations. The crowd, unfortunately, hadn't let up, even as the Chinese men attempted to move on. The men continued to be vocal, adding pushes and shoves to the tormenting.

"Fellas...we should send them Chinamen back home," a man added to the fracas.

"Yeah...in a box!"

Danny recognized that last man. It was one of the Roberts Boys. At the man's shoulder was another member of the Roberts Boys. As Danny walked by, the two Roberts Boys noticed him, made eye contact with him, and nudged each other. They began to peel away from the crowd as Danny returned to Stephen and Albert.

Not wanting to appear alarmed, Danny whispered to Stephen as he prepared to mount his horse that he had just seen two of the Roberts Boys. But before they could even decide what to do, the decision was made for them. Walking toward them with a quickened pace were the two men. One of them had a pick handle resting on his shoulder.

"Well, well, well...I'd never thought you two woulda made it dis far," the man with the pick handle said, an edge of cockiness in his voice. "I took ya for quitters."

Trying to diffuse the situation, Danny raised his hands shoulder height, saying, "Listen, mister...I don't know what you and your friend have against us, but we have no quarrel with any of you."

The man and his partner walked closer to the boys and their wagon. There was a swagger to their approach as if to say they knew they were intimidating and were used to getting what they wanted.

"There ain't nothin' protectin' ya now," the other man chimed in, "No Kinney...no boss-man...nothin'."

Some of the small crowd that was taunting the Chinese men noticed the intensifying situation between the Roberts Boys and the Two Hens group. Losing interest in the Chinese, they switched their attention to the new, potential conflict, leaving in twos and threes, until there was nobody left to harass the Chinese men. Seeing a chance for escape, the Chinese men slipped away.

Albert, not having a history with the Roberts Boys, didn't realize what was going on. All he saw was the growing crowd and believed that a fight was imminent. He was in the wagon amidst the supplies, arranging items to better secure them, when Danny had returned from the postal agent. Outnumbered, Albert contemplated grabbing Danny's shotgun that was under a tarp.

It appeared to be a do-or-die situation. Danny, Stephen, and Albert just wanted to leave and go about their business.

"Look...we're just leaving," Stephen added. "We'll just be on our way. No harm...no foul."

The Roberts Boys would have none of that. Full of liquor and fight, these men wanted to make Danny and Stephen bleed. They wanted to hurt them; make them understand, physically, that the Roberts Boys could do what they wanted, when they wanted.

The man with the wooden handle took it off his shoulder and pointed it at Danny. "Naw...you ain't goin' nowhere. You owe us satisfaction." He poked the handle into Danny's shoulder to punctuate what he was saying.

Danny took a deep breath to steady his nerves. The last thing he needed at the moment was to antagonize this man and provoke him further. He wasn't a coward, but he saw very little point in fighting this man armed with what amounted to a club. The tension, however, was nearing an apex. Oddly enough, Danny's body felt loose. His muscles and tendons weren't tight and bound up like a man who was scared.

"This doesn't have to happen," Stephen said with an elevated voice.

Ignored and confused, Albert shouted from the back of the wagon, "What the Hell's going on? We've done nothin' to you!"

The man with the handle snapped his attention to Albert, not noticing him before. He also saw the hens and the rooster in their crates on the buckboard.

"Hey, Harry! This boy's still playin' with chickens! Remember what happened last time?" He and his friend laughed.

"Sure do, George!" Harry responded. "I think that boy owes Eli a chicken or two."

Agreeing with his friend, George moved closer to the chickens on the wagon. Using the handle, he punched at the chicken crates, saying, "I think we'll be taking these chickens...maybe some flour..."

But he didn't have a chance to finish his statement. Danny had enough of his talk. It was one thing for George, this Roberts Boy, to run his mouth and throw his weight around. However, he was now threatening to take Danny's property; the investment for the future.

Before the man even knew what happened, Danny drew back his right arm, his fingers bunched tight into a mini anvil. His body pivoted on his left foot to transfer all of his strength, his body force, through the arm and fist that was slicing through the air. As George's mouth finished saying the word "flour," Danny's assault caught him on the left side of his jaw. The punch was devastating. George's eyes immediately rolled back, his knees buckled, and he crumbled to the ground.

Shocked, Harry stood there momentarily before lunging toward Danny. But he had no real chance to get at Danny. Acting on instinct, Stephen caught Harry by the arm and began slugging him in the face. Two punches and Harry's nose was bleeding. A third punch dropped him to the ground. Stephen and Danny had spent the last year building muscle and grit. In a fair match, they could more than hold their own.

Getting up, blood trickling from his nose, Harry looked to the gathered crowd shouting, "Get them! You saw it...they jumped us!"

Danny and Stephen, adrenaline pumping and flush with victory, couldn't stand down a crowd. Maybe they could take one or two of the mob, but not all of them. Nobody could do that, even with Albert's help. Luckily, it didn't come to that.

The leader of the mob, the so-called Vigilance Committee, looked at the unconscious George and bleeding Harry. He shook his head and chuckled a bit.

"Seems to me that you two gents went looking for trouble and found more than you bargained for," the leader said to Harry. He walked over to George, knelt, and rolled George onto his side.

"These men had no issue with you. Fact is, you came at them with a club. It wasn't a fair fight...you started it...they finished it." He stood up and walked to Harry and grasped him by the arm to further emphasize his words. "Son...It's one thing to mess with the Celestials, but when you threaten a man's property and wellbeing...well, then you're just asking for a beating."

Looking to Danny, Stephen, and Albert the man recommended, "I think it's best you boys move along now. Far as I can see, you've done nothing wrong."

Nodding their agreement to the man, Stephen mounted his horse, and Danny and Albert led the oxen down the street toward the edge of town. As they exited Sacramento, Danny stopped the rig and grabbed his loaded shotgun. He carried that weapon firmly all the way back to camp.

For the first mile, they walked on in silence. Then Albert looked over to Danny, stating with a crooked smile on his face, "Remind me to never make you mad."

They had a good laugh over that statement, and Danny and Stephen explained their brief history with the Roberts Boys. Their adrenaline faded, and they marched on. For three days, though, they periodically looked over their shoulders.

***

Over the next few months, business continued as usual, despite the periodic heavy rains that virtually shut down mining activities. When it wasn't raining, men feverishly worked. Everyone had a certain hustle about their work. Mining sites were claimed, test holes were panned, and if they proved fruitful enough, then the men stayed on to exploit the claim. Otherwise, they moved on. The same was true for the Two Hens Company. Two of their claims were productive, so, they continued to work on them. Seeing that the other two claims weren't worth the effort, they pulled down their markers and staked two more claims in likely locations near their camp.

Danny was especially busy, but not working the earth. He was hoping to soon work the miners with Julia Banks. The day after the boys returned from Sacramento, Danny hitched the team and brought the supplies over to the Banks' camp. Carl and his brother were still trying their hand at mining, having a little more success than before. Julia was, as usual, trying to carve a home from the rugged location. That energy would soon be allocated to carving a business from the men on the North Fork of the American River. Danny unloaded the goods, went over what he had bought, and then spent the next fifteen minutes listening to Julia proudly review the types of dishes she could prepare. She was a charming woman, six years older than Danny. And beautiful, too. She had a certain toughness hidden amidst her delicate features and an independent strength that made her confident and ambitious. Julia was the kind of woman that Danny hoped to meet someday. Danny knew that Carl was a lucky man.

Together, Julia and Danny plotted on the ground what they planned. In two days she planned to open her kitchen. Until then, time would be spent preparing the site. Initially, it would be a pretty rough establishment, with no structure other than a tarp secured to trees to provide shelter from the elements, and stumps to be used as seats. Julia would prepare meals in her Dutch ovens using an open fire. Her customers would be required to bring their own plates, but that was a small inconvenience for a home-cooked meal prepared by a lovely woman. For one to two dollars a meal, men could avoid having to cook, and, if just for a short time, imagine they were back home.

Although Danny worked every morning with the Two Hens Company, he spent the afternoons helping Julia prepare for business. On the mile-and-a-half walk to the Banks' camp each day, Danny made sure to hit every camp between his own and his destination. He'd stop and shoot the breeze, but always find a way to advertise Julia's business. He'd say, "Did you hear there's a pretty lady selling supper down the trail? She's only charging one to two dollars in gold dust!" or he'd talk about the dishes she was planning—stews, pot pies, beans and cornbread, flapjacks. Danny left them dreaming and drooling.

That first evening, under a hand-painted sign that read "Julia's Kitchen," she served eight men beef stew and cornbread, taking in eight dollars in dust. The next evening there were fifteen men to eat flapjacks and bacon. Seventeen men sat down for supper the next evening. And on it went. Julia's cooking was proof enough that the gold exchanged for a meal was worth it. Danny continued to advertise the kitchen, telling strangers about the service and posting signs at trailheads. Men who'd eaten at the kitchen passed the word on themselves.

Short of a week, Danny's initial investment was recovered, and there was no sign at all that the customer base would decline. Danny had to make another trip to Sacramento for double the amount of supplies. He also saw no sign of the Roberts Boys, which was a relief. Business was booming for all involved. Per the request of numerous men, Julia began to serve breakfast, too. There was no way Danny could keep up with the amount of supplies needed, so, he worked his connections in Sacramento to pay a modest fee to have supplies delivered to the site of Julia's Kitchen.

It wasn't long before Carl and David Banks realized that mining wasn't for them. Julia was making more money each day than they were each week. Business expansion was the only logical step for the family. Danny helped the two men build a proper log dining room...and then a saloon...and then a small boarding house. Danny still had a sixty percent stake in Julia's Kitchen, but the other business enterprises were solely owned by the Banks family. All three businesses complimented each other; all three businesses were mutually beneficial. The gamble was golden.

Winter turned to spring, spring to summer, and summer to fall. California was admitted as the 31st state in the Union, and the Two Hens Company was still turning a profit, earning each of the four members over $6,000 each. Danny's growing yard of chickens was producing more eggs than ever before. Those hens also produced new chickens that he added to the production line or were sold to Julia for meat. And Danny's investment in Julia's

Kitchen was producing him a clear profit of over $4,000. Life was good, and time marched on.

1851 brought much of the same thing—prosperity. But the number of people flooding into California had increased. The business was even more profitable for Julia and her family, as well as for Danny Vance and his connection to the Kitchen. But the claims for the Two Hens Company were playing out. As their diggings turned less profitable, their new claims ranged farther and farther away from their base camp. Placer gold was becoming more difficult to find, and miners pushed farther up the creeks, rivers, and ravines.

Danny was finding the thought of mining month after month less and less attractive. It wasn't the work that bothered him, as evident from the sweat equity he'd put into everything he did. What bothered him was the uncertainty of the whole endeavor. There may be gold. There may be enough to cover costs and make a profit. There may be any number of possible outcomes. Although it pained him to do so, Danny decided to exit the Two Hens Mining Company. Stephen, Jeremiah, and Albert understood Danny's perspective. They also understood that Danny's profits from Julia's Kitchen only continued to increase. Cashing out, Danny took a cut of the Company's profits amounting to $7,500. With no hard feelings and the very real chance that they'd see each other again soon, the boys traveled on to stake new claims on richer ground. Danny stayed on at the cabin, thinking about his next move.

***

Danny's time at the cabin was a lonely experience. He was used to the company of his partners, even if most of that time together was spent toiling. Solitude is something certain individuals revel in and crave. Danny didn't mind being alone for a while, but soon, the visits from passing miners on the way to the diggings pushed him to spend more time with the Banks family.

The boarding house, saloon, and restaurant proved to be worth more than any claim the Two Hens or the Banks family had ever worked. The rough log structure that was initially constructed for their business was replaced with lumber from a sawmill. Patrons were no longer required to bring their own plates, cups, and utensils. All of that was provided now. The family also hired several Chinese workers to wash dishes, clean rooms, and do laundry. By all accounts, they were successful, and by proxy, Danny was successful. But Danny was restless. His revenue stream from Julia's Kitchen was because of his initial investment. It didn't sit well with Danny that he still reaped the rewards from that original deal, but his money was no longer needed for Julia's Kitchen…he knew it, and Julia knew it. Julia, to her credit, still felt indebted to Danny. His vision and investment led to all that she and her family had. She had a certain affinity for Danny, as did the rest of her family.

But fair is fair. Danny wished to revise their deal. Over Julia's objections, he renegotiated, leaving her with eighty percent of the profits. Additionally, Danny insisted that the Banks family take his chickens and keep them as their own. It was Danny's way of feeling connected to the business and justifying the profits he'd receive. Doing this also allowed him to travel the region since the responsibility for maintaining the coop was no longer holding him back.

As 1851 progressed toward 1852, things were changing in the region. Simple placer mining was still practiced but with shrinking profitability. Companies with more financing hired large numbers of laborers to divert creeks and streams, even portions of rivers, to gain access to gold-bearing gravel and sand. Individual miners still struck it rich, but not as often in the first year or two of the Rush. Some companies didn't mine at all. Instead, they made their fortunes building small wooden flumes to deliver water long distances to dry diggings. Once again, one man's need was another man's profit.

Small towns continued to sprout around the newest gold strike, and then disappear into obscurity as newer strikes were announced and miners rushed off to better opportunities. The population in the mining region increased, the demand for goods continued, and the need to transport people and materials persisted. Danny had a gut feeling that he was on the cusp of additional success. His entrepreneurial spirit urged him to visit Sacramento.

In the winter of 1851-1852, Danny came down out of the hills with a mule he'd purchased, extra clothes, personal items, rations for the trip, and over $15,000 in gold dust and nuggets, gold and silver coins, and banknotes. There were many options for lodging, but Danny had a specific place in mind to stay called the Fish House. Located in a residential section of town, it was a boarding house with an attached dining room and a contract with a nearby stable for guests to board their horses and mules. The Fish House was reasonably priced and in a quiet area, far enough from the saloons, dance halls, and opera houses to avoid the riff-raff of the bustling town. The entertainment district was within walking distance, though, if Danny felt adventurous.

Once washed up and settled in, Danny visited one of the more prominent and respectable banks in town. Having sold gold to the operators, he trusted the institution, but his faith had increased even more since the bank's investors recently installed a fireproof vault. Even if Danny believed he could hold his own in a fair fight, having over $15,000 in wealth on his person was insane. Danny opened an account and deposited $12,500. Working with the manager of the bank, Danny arranged to send $2,000 back to his folks, hoping that it'd help his mother and father pay off their bills and allow Seth to buy a fancy new rifle. He kept five hundred dollars on hand to pay for his incidentals while in town. Before concluding his business, he informed the manager that Julia Banks on the American River would send a deposit for his account once a month.

For three days, Danny took in the town. He had no real idea what he wanted to do, as of yet. Danny went to the theater one evening, finding the entertainment a wonderful diversion. Another afternoon he went down to the docks to watch people embark and disembark from a variety of vessels. It wasn't that he was bored, but he was getting there. He was spending time walking, people-watching, looking in storefront windows, and just doing a whole lot of nothing. Danny was impressed with the variety of shops and services obtainable in the growing town of Sacramento.

On his third day back in Sacramento, Danny was walking down the sidewalk of a crowded commercial district. It was rather busy with both foot traffic and wagons, and the sounds of business being conducted were equated to progress. Compared to the neighborhood where the Fish House was located, this was an especially loud area.

Crossing the street, Danny heard a faint call, "Daniel...Daniel!"

Looking around, Danny couldn't pinpoint who was calling, or even if it was someone beckoning him. He slowed his pace and continued across the street, but he pivoted on the balls of his feet to look around.

"Daniel...Daniel Vance!" working his way through the crowd was a familiar face. Over six foot tall, weathered, with a well-groomed, but full mustache...it was Jim Kinney. Danny, elated to see an old friend, briskly finished crossing the street, and mounted the sidewalk with a spry little hop. Kinney had a noticeable limp, but other than that, it was the same old Jim Kinney. The two men shook hands and warmly embraced each other in greeting, like long-lost relatives meeting at a chance encounter.

Jim firmly held Danny by the shoulders, looking him up and down. "Just look at you! You've all grown up! How ya been? Where's ya partner...Stephen was his name, I believe."

"Things have gone well. I ain't much of a miner, but I gave it a go. Made most of my money off those chickens and trading goods," Danny said as both men moved to the edge of the sidewalk to avoid being an obstruction to the other pedestrians.

"You sure mothered those chickens...'spose they done returned the favor," Kinney said with a little chuckle.

"Sure enough. As far as Stephen goes, he's still up in the hills with Jeremiah and Albert Swanson."

"Good men, those three. Always hard workers, at least on the trail...well, I guess in the diggins' too! What say you and I go get a drink and catch up?" Kinney suggested.

Danny readily agreed with the suggestion. His throat was dry and he had nowhere to be. They went into the nearest saloon, The Elephant. It was an aptly named establishment. Many a patron came to see the elephant, only to wind up at a table or the bar in that building. In a sense, whether or not they found success, if they had a drink there they'd seen The Elephant. Kinney and Danny found an empty table in the back. A smart-looking man wearing saloonkeeper's garb—sleeve garters, white apron, and all—took their order of two whiskeys, went behind the bar, and returned promptly with their order. The men nodded their thanks and Danny paid for their drinks. And with that, the men were left to catch up.

Over the next hour, and another drink, the friends talked about their lives over the last two years. Danny relayed his partnership in the Two Hens Mining Company, their success and decline, his investment in Julia's Kitchen, the run-in with two of the Roberts Boys, and his eventual decision to come down from the hills to Sacramento to find something new to do.

Like Danny, Jim Kinney had also experienced much in his short time in California. He and a few other men from the Ohio Boys chose to go to the Southern mines. He found moderate success, but compared to the Middle and

North Forks of the American River, the area was relatively dry, requiring men to either haul dirt to a water source or bring the water to the diggings. It was difficult work, just like any other type of mining. Kinney talked of his multiple claims, some good, others bad, and news of other members of the Ohio Boys. A few had struck it rich and were now living the high life in San Francisco. Several had given up and returned home to Ohio. At least one was rumored to have been shanghaied and was toiling away on a ship working the China trade. One man was hanged for jumping a claim, one was shot in a dispute, three had died from various causes, and one man had drowned. Kinney himself flirted with disaster, breaking his left leg when he took a tumble down a hillside in the spring of 1851. Unfortunately, it never quite set right, resulting in the permanent limp he was now sporting. But that was a turning point in his life. He moved to Sacramento, sent for his wife, purchased a small home, and was now in the process of growing his own freighting business. He had four wagons and oxen teams, as well as five men under his employ. His wasn't a business of purchasing supplies for the camps. He was solely interested in delivering said supplies for his paying customers.

As with many a man who'd come to California, Danny included, Kinney was looking toward bigger and better opportunities. As placer mining became more difficult and the population continued to grow, men moved on far and wide for new pay dirt. This was a great thing for men in Kinney's line of work. The greater the distance from towns, the greater the need for teamsters and mule-skinners. It was a winning formula for a man like Kinney. But his prosperity was limited by the amount of freight he could haul. With just four wagons, he was only able to reach a certain number of destinations at any given time. Kinney dreamed of expanding the number of rigs he had to at least eight, and he also desired to add a string of mules to transport supplies to camps way off the beaten path. The only thing holding him back was the lack of funds.

Thinking the situation over, Danny was intrigued with the possibility of becoming an investor and partner in Kinney's business. All of the circumstances seemed right. Kinney was a reliable man, and he knew his trade. The population of California was continually growing, and people were always on the move. They'd need goods, wherever they were, and the goods had to be transported by someone. Danny had a sizeable amount of money secured in the bank, and he'd have a residual income from Julia's Kitchen each month to keep him afloat if need be.

With their drinks finished, the two men walked to Kinney's shop—a barn-like structure with an office, a blacksmith's station, and a corral for his stock. All of his men, save for the Smitty, were out on runs. The shop was clean and organized, with plenty of room for expansion. And, if the other employees were as competent and affable as

Eugene, the blacksmith, then Kinney's operation was off to a great start.

Since the day was getting on, Jim invited Danny to his home to meet his wife and join them for supper. Perhaps Kinney was pulling out all the stops to wrangle Danny as an investor. Or maybe it was because he genuinely liked the young man. Either way, it didn't matter much to Danny, for he was his own man and made his own decisions. He'd grown to trust his instincts, especially when it came to business opportunities. He saw the potential and believed that it was a sound prospect. Danny wanted to be involved; meeting Mrs. Kinney and having supper was a bonus.

They continued to talk about what could be done with increased investment over dinner, much to the chagrin of Mrs. Kinney. Standing just over five feet tall, she was a stout woman, with a demeanor and gentle nature that reminded Danny a lot of his mother. He missed her a great deal, so Mrs. Kinney's company filled his heart with joy.

Jim Kinney continued to talk about his business, stating, "If you came onboard, your investment would provide a healthy boost...we could give the competition somethin' to think about...you never know, maybe even get a boat or two to open up transport between Sacramento and San Francisco."

Mrs. Kinney was becoming irritated with her husband, as evidenced by her interjection. "Now Jim...let the poor boy eat. You know I don't favor business at the table."

Turning to Danny, she apologetically said, "You'll have to excuse my husband...he often forgets how to act when guests are around the table."

Mrs. Kinney's reprimand of her husband was endearing. She patted Danny's hand with her own. "Now Danny, dear...I bet you'd like a piece of apple pie." Her chair made a slight scraping sound as she scooted it from the table to stand up and go to the kitchen.

"I'm sorry Danny...I guess I get to thinking an dreamin'...that little lady in there keeps my feet on the ground."

"Jim," Danny wiped his mouth with his cloth napkin, "You've got my support...I'll invest."

Jim was relieved to hear Danny say that. In Jim's estimation, it was a winning situation for all involved. He was eager to get started, but it could wait until tomorrow. For now, he'd enjoy his food and coffee, and the company of his new partner. He'd also refrain from talking business; Mrs. Kinney's reprimand was more than a suggestion.

***

It didn't take long for Jim and Danny to come to a financial agreement. In exchange for Danny's $8,000 investment, he'd become a fifty percent working partner. There was an emphasis on the title of "working partner." It was expected that Danny would involve himself in every aspect of the business, and Danny wouldn't want it any other way. With the injection of Danny's investment, they were able to make some upgrades within a few days. Four more wagons were purchased from newly arrived emigrants, as were enough oxen to operate the rigs. They also purchased all that was needed to outfit the rigs—ropes, tarps, extra yokes and wagon parts, feed, and lumber to build taller sideboards. Some of the money was used to purchase four tickets from San Francisco to Sacramento to bring in merchants to meet with the partners, examine the facilities, and hopefully negotiate contracts for freighting. The men also met with representatives of larger mining companies to discuss contracts for hauling gear and supplies. As more contracts were secured, in addition to the five men already employed by the J. Kinney Freighting Co., six more employees were hired.

The J. Kinney Freighting Co., already moderately successful, steadily expanded its clientele and areas serviced. By the summer of 1853, the company's wagons and mules carried goods at one time or another to various mining camps, close by Sacramento and far-flung—Goodyears Bar, Rough and Ready, Dutch Flat, Gold Run, Fiddletown, Jackass Hill, Angels Camp, Chinese Camp...and many others. Every man with an interest in the company, employee and owner, loaded and unloaded freight, and went on runs.

Danny was able to pick up a route that went up the American River every two weeks to Julia's Kitchen and the family's boarding house and saloon, delivering dry goods, barreled and bottled liquors, canned items, and whatever it was that was ordered. Delivering freight was often a monotonous, even tedious task, but making his delivery to the Banks family was the highlight of his week. The time he spent with the family, especially Julia, was special to him. He respected the marital union of Carl and Julia, but it was difficult to convince himself that he wasn't smitten with Julia. She was always pleasant, and that smile was engaging. He was also sure that she carried a well-hidden torch for him. But commitments meant something to Danny, and boundaries were meant to be respected.

Life settled into a new, but now familiar, pattern for Danny. Contracts and agreements were made, freighting manifests were drawn up, items were loaded and secured, and teams were sent on their way. Eating, working, and sleeping day after day as the months passed. Letters were written home, and news from home was joyfully read. It was an existence based on routine; not unpleasant, and not overbearing. Danny could compare his scheduled life to a feeling of comfort, like being in a feather-stuffed bed under a warm blanket on a cold, wintery life. Watching his bank account grow probably didn't make Danny want to alter his reality either. Rarely will profit push a man away.

For the freighting company, every week and every month was financially better than the last. Their prediction that the need for dependable, competitively priced freighting would increase in demand was accurate and fruitful. The story for placer miners was not as predictable, nor was it as lucrative as it once was. By the end of 1852, larger mining companies were displacing individual miners and smaller companies, purchasing claims, and consolidating their influence and power. And the techniques employed were also changing from placer mining to hard-rock mining. This involved digging shafts into mountains, rock ledges, and the ground to follow veins of gold-bearing quartz. It was labor-intensive and expensive, necessitating large amounts of capital just to reach the quartz.

Removed from the shafts and pits, mined rocks were then crushed, sometimes with Spanish arrastras. First used in the 1500s by Spanish miners, an arrastra consisted of three main parts—a circular track lined with flat stones on the bottom and the side; two large, flat but round, stones with holes in their center where an axel was attached; and a central pivot where two mules or horses could be attached. The process used with the arrastra was rather simple. Ore was placed in the track, and the drag stones on the pivot were repeatedly dragged over the ore, crushing it into a course powder-like material. Liquid mercury, or quicksilver, was added to the material and the grinding process continued. The gold in the coarse material joined with the quicksilver, amalgamated as it was called, and water was added to the mixture to float out the lighter material. More ore was added to the arrastra, pulverized, and quicksilver added. This process would continue over a week or two until the amalgamated substance was collected and then processed. Sometimes the mercury was partially separated from the gold by straining the amalgam through chamois. The remaining mercury was heated in a retort, with the vaporized mercury collected as it passed through a tube. What remained was the gold.

But more efficient, and quicker, was the use of a stamp mill. The same concept held with the mill—the goal was to crush ore to aid in the extraction of the embedded veins of gold from the other minerals. Instead of dragging stones to pulverize the rock, the mill used a series of heavy metal stamps that were housed in a wooden battery. Using water or steam power, the stamps were rapidly raised and lowered using a drive shaft and cam, wielding a great deal of force that demolished rock. The powdered slurry was spread across a mercury-coated copper plate or recovery table, and, just like with the arrastra, the end product was amalgamated gold that was further processed and separated from the mercury.

Another gold-recovery method that began to see widespread use by 1853 was hydraulic mining. Its first use is credited to Edward Matteson. Using high-pressure water hoses to wash down hillsides, debris flowed into Long Toms with ridges coated with quicksilver. Large numbers of laborers operated the system on all its levels. This was a destructive method, causing erosion and clogging streams and rivers with leftover slurry. That's not to mention the poisoning of the ecosystem from the unclaimed mercury used in this and all the methods using amalgamation.

Regardless of the evolving mining technique, food and supplies still needed to be delivered to the camps. The dismantled machinery itself, and the massive amounts of toxic mercury stored in large flasks, also required the use of freighting companies. These companies became the lifeline for isolated camps, supply depots, and boomtowns. It was a bountiful business to be invested in, but growth demanded new routes. And just like placer miners whose ears perked at the sound of a new strike, the J. Kinney Freighting Co. kept its ear to the ground for the chance to exploit untapped or underserved areas. Theirs was a proven formula. So, when word came north of a new strike far to the south, outside the confines of the Sacramento River Valley and the western slopes of the Sierra Nevada Mountains, it piqued Danny and Jim's interest, as well as miners looking for the next big thing.

Chapter 8
The Lure South

————◆————

M iners were a peculiar sort of men. At one moment a miner might be working a moderately successful claim, making over sixteen dollars a day. But a rumor of a rich strike, often unsubstantiated, could start a human flood. Productive claims were abandoned, and a new race to stake pay-dirt was on. All in the quest for more—more opportunity; more gold; more chances to see the elephant. And it was that rumor of gold in the Kern River country that began a new rush to that region. It was just a trickle of people at first, but a wave of 5,000 people at its height.

The first miners in the Southern San Joaquin Valley and the Kern River region weren't seeking the luster of gold, they sought wealth in the form of pelts. Trespassers on land first claimed by Spain, and then inherited by Mexico, fur trappers crisscrossed the region throughout the 1820s and 1830s. Jedidiah Smith, Kit Carson, Alexis Godey, Joseph R. Walker, and others searched for abundant sources of fur-bearing animals. Like so many miners in the 1850s, these trappers might have experienced success in the beginning, but they eventually moved on to explore new ground.

More trespassers arrived in the 1840s. The United States Army, Corps of Topographical Engineers, led by Captain John C. Fremont, entered the region in 1844 and 1845. The unauthorized exploration of foreign soil by agents of the United States government was a questionable move. Maybe it was done purely in the name of scientific exploration and to further map the North American continent. It is also possible that the party's purpose was designed to pave the way for the acquisition of the West from Mexico. Either way, Fremont's group entered the Kern River Valley and explored parts of the North and South forks of the Kern River, as well as portions of the Kern River Canyon. It was a member of a later Fremont expedition that found a small amount of gold on the Kern River in 1851. It wasn't enough gold to cause a rush, but rumors of its presence set some men to thinking.

Fueling the speculation of gold outside the Mother Lode country was the story of a Spanish doctor who was supposedly the only survivor of a group of miners who found an area of immense wealth somewhere along the waters of the Kern River. Golden nuggets were spread across the riverbed, and the hills and outcroppings of rock were chock-full of the glittering mineral. As with many stories of lost mines, the doctor was the only survivor of an Indian attack on the group, and he couldn't accurately detail where the area was. But just the chance that it existed was enough to entice some men to the Kern River; men who weren't satisfied with their present situation...men who were driven by the desire for more. Some of these men found traces of placer gold along the river, enough to keep their interest and feed their fever for the next big strike, but, again, not enough to draw a rush of miners.

By 1853, the J. Kinney Freighting Co. was periodically delivering goods to the small town of Visalia using the Stockton-Los Angeles Road. It was there that agents for the company heard the news that a sizeable amount of placer gold was found in early 1854. Near the top and bottom of Greenhorn Gulch along Greenhorn Creek (a seasonal creek that emptied into the Kern), almost at the same time, two groups of miners found enough placer gold to cause a stir. This announcement sparked a rush, bringing miners and entrepreneurs to the Kern River country. Not long after and within ten or so miles, another strike was proclaimed by Richard M. Keyes, leading to the founding of a small town called Keyesville. Men, old hands and those new to mining, from the Mother Lode region and the sleepy pueblo of Los Angeles, prepared for their journey and planned how they'd spend their fortunes. Their lust drove them to this new strike. Their lust also brought the J. Kinney Freighting Co., and Danny Vance, to the Kern River.

***

Freighting goods to Visalia from Sacramento and Stockton was a relatively straightforward task. The biggest obstacle was Tulare Lake. Depending on the amount of rain and snow, Tulare Lake encompassed between 570 and 690 square miles, making it the largest freshwater lake west of the Mississippi River. Filled by the Kern, Tule, Kaweah, and portions of the Kings Rivers, Tule Lake spread from the Buena Vista and Goose Lakes in the Southern San Joaquin Valley all the way north to the San Joaquin River. Along its edges, clogged with Tule rushes and marsh grasses, deer, elk, and antelope lived. In the water itself, an abundant number of waterfowl stopped over as part of the Pacific Flyway, and numerous species of fish, including Chinook salmon, brought the lake alive. It was a sportsman's paradise, first bringing bands of Yokuts to its shores, and then those of European descent.

Before the California Gold Rush, the San Joaquin Valley itself was sparsely populated by non-Indians, with the majority of the Spanish and Mexican Land Grants established west of the Coastal Ranges. The large ranchos focused on raising cattle for their hides and tallow to trade to American shipcaptains in exchange for manufactured goods. There wasn't much to entice the population into the valley. Access to the Pacific Ocean, and proximity to one of the twenty-one missions, was a lifeline that acted as a barrier to further settlement.

The acquisition of California by the United States and the California Gold Rush reset the lines of settlement. The population broke free of the coast and moved east. As the population of miners and settlers pushed South from Sacramento, the migration had no choice but to straddle the eastern shore of Tulare Lake and the foothills of the western slope of the Sierra Nevada Mountains. And thus, was the route of the Stockton-Los Angeles Road.

The Road, however, wasn't absent of some difficulties. There were numerous creeks, drainages, and rivers that had to be crossed. Depending on the time of year, several of these waterways were dry or could be forded with ease. But when the rains came or snow in the Sierras melted, the only way to traverse the San Joaquin, Stanislaus, Tuolumne, Merced, Mariposa, Kings, and Kern Rivers was by ferry. Other than these obstacles, the road running from Sacramento to Visalia, via Stockton, was remarkably well-maintained and well-traveled. Freight and emigrant wagons had very little difficulty moving goods and people. Where the story begins to change, though, is the road, and subsequent trail, from Visalia to the new claims in the Kern River Valley and Canyon.

The trip from Visalia to the Kern River diggings was essentially a three-phased journey—Visalia to Linn's Valley; Linn's Valley up to the ridges of the Greenhorn Mountains; and from the ridges down the eastern slopes to the diggings. The sixty-eight miles from Visalia to Linn's Valley was noted as being fairly adequate as far as travel standards go. The road made its way through the grassy foothills and oak and brush-covered mountains, crossing washouts and coulees as it lazily climbed in elevation. A handsome place where feed was plentiful, Linn's Valley would, in time, also become a supply depot of sorts for those headed to the Kern River mines or to the mines on the high desert.

But from Linn's Valley on, the trip was nothing short of miserable. The Greenhorn Trail, as it was called, wound its way from Linn's Valley down through Poso Flats. From there, the Trail faced the steep sides of the Greenhorn Mountains. Those who cut the path had no choice but to break a winding trail up one of the serpentine ridges to where the road traveled a short distance on comparably flat ground before dropping down into the Kern River Canyon. Rarely fit for wagons or coaches, most of the traffic on the Greenhorn Trail was by foot or mule pack train. No person would describe that path as one that was easy. Dreaded was, perhaps, a better description.

However, clearing the top of Greenhorn to where it made its way down to the diggings wasn't any easier. The steep descent, using switchbacks and runs down ridges was tough on man and beast. Teamsters who managed to drag a wagon up the Greenhorn Trail from Poso Flat now faced the very real threat that the wagon, gear and all, could break free of the mules or oxen and topple down the mountain. Men chained the back wheels of their wagons to slow progress. Others attached logs to the back of the wagon, the thought being that dragging logs would decrease the speed of the wagon as it threatened to rocket down the trail. Many clever teamsters attached wagon shoes—twelve-inch iron sleds—to the rear wheels to reduce the wear and tear sliding down the rough trail could have on the wagon wheels.

As one can imagine, getting to the Kern River diggings was an endeavor many men suffered through. They eagerly spread along the Kern River, up and down the numerous little creek beds and small canyons chasing their dreams. Arriving and actively prospecting were one thing, maintaining a stock of supplies, tools, and food was an entirely different story. And that is what kept the J. Kenney Freighting Co. and others just like it in business.

***

"Gonzales and Thompson just got back from their run to Visalia," Jim Kinney stated as Danny walked into the office of the J. Kinney Freighting Co. Jim was seated at a table reviewing paperwork, part of the responsibilities of running a business. As unexciting as it was, it was necessary, and it did give the partners an accurate sense of their business growth.

Danny hung his hat on a hook on the wall, walked over to the stove, picked up the coffee pot by the handle with a rag, and grabbed a cup.

"They have any problems?" Danny asked as he finished pouring coffee into his cup. Before replacing the pot, he lifted it in a motion to Jim.

Jim lifted his cup, "Please...no problems at all. Smooth as expected, but they did hear some interestin' news of a new strike."

Interested in what Kinney had to say, Danny topped off Jim's cup, replaced the pot on the stove, and walked over to the table to have a seat in one of the empty chairs.

"You don't say? Where abouts?" Danny asked between sips of coffee.

Jim pulled a series of maps from a nearby shelf, shuffled through them, and opened the correct one showing the Southern Sierra Nevada Mountains.

"Right in this general area," his finger made a circular motion on one side of the Greenhorn Mountains.

Intrigued, Danny looked closely at the map, noting the location's distance from Sacramento, Stockton, and Visalia.

"Looks like some rugged country. Is it verified?"

"As verified as most rumors are, I suppose." Kinney took a sip of his coffee and set the cup down. "Might be worth checking out."

The men agreed that there was no harm in asking around about the strike on the Kern River. The worst thing that could happen was nothing. With any luck, someone would validate the rumors and a merchant would contract with the company to haul supplies to the region.

That afternoon, they visited several gold buyers, two saloons, and two merchants. Some of the patrons shared what they'd heard over a glass of whiskey, confirming the fractured rumors brought back from Visalia. It was information, but not certifiable. Jim and Danny left the saloons with no more information than they already had. Their heads were feeling the slight effects of the watered-down whiskey, though.

The gold buyers, however, were well-informed. They confirmed that the rumors were, in fact, true. They weren't aware of how big the strike was, or the quality of the gold, but their sources were reliable. They believed in the claims and seemed excited. The gold buyers each speculated about sending an agent down to the region to assess the finds and purchase the precious minerals.

That was good enough for the partners of the J. Kinney Freighting Co. If the gold merchants were confident enough to send out an agent, then the company would actively seek a freighting contract. That is where the visits to the merchants came into play. The J. Kinney Freighting Co. wasn't in the business of selling goods. They just hauled them. Jim and Danny paid a visit to two merchants that maintained freighting contracts with the company to feel them out on the situation on the find to the south. Theirs was a bigger gamble if they chose to ship supplies to the region. Whether or not there were customers to buy their wares, they'd still have to pay the freighting fees. So, both of them were cautious. It was a big investment and a gamble...they could reap more profits by securing new customers. But they needed time to explore the opportunity and run the numbers. They both promised to get back to Jim and Danny in a few days. That was the best the men could hope for at the moment. They'd have to bide their time for an answer.

In the meantime, business continued as usual. Danny continued his usual routine and went on his delivery run up the American River. For old times' sake, he took a short detour up Shirttail Creek to see the original camp of the Two Hens Mining Company. The camp hadn't changed much except for the residents. A small family was now occupying the log cabin, working the abandoned mines and tailings to scratch out a meager living. This wasn't uncommon. An abandoned claim is typically free for the taking. Danny visited with the new family, telling them the history of the place and he walked around and pointed particulars out. Knowing that they weren't there for his pleasure, he bid his farewell, rolling the memories of his time with the Two Hens around in his mind. As he headed to the Banks' place he wondered what his former partners were up to and where they were. He decided he would seek them out someday soon.

Pulling into the Banks' place he found the place as busy as it usually was. Men were in the saloon, boarders were registered, and Julia's Kitchen was preparing to open. Danny and a few of the Chinese workers employed by the Banks family unloaded the supplies in the backyard. When finished, he sought out Julia. Typically, she would greet him when he arrived, but not today. She was in the kitchen doing meal prep. It was almost as if she were avoiding Danny, but he couldn't imagine that to be the case. Walking into the kitchen through the back door, Danny found Julia.

"Good day to you, Mrs. Banks," Danny playfully said in the most formal way he could muster.

Julia turned toward Danny, wiping her hands on the apron. She smiled and acted surprised to see him.

"And good day to you," she said with an over-empha-sized curtsey.

"I was wondering where...." Danny stopped midsen-tence, noticing a red mark on the side of Julia's face and a slight swelling about the outside of her left eye.

"Oh...it's nothing," Julia averted her eyes out of embar-rassment and shame.

Danny walked to Julia, took her chin delicately into his hand, and turned her head.

"That doesn't look like nothing," genuine concern in his voice.

She reached up, grasping his hand to remove it from her chin. She held his hand a moment longer than was necessary. A bolt of lightning shot up his arm, but his heart sank and anger rose when he saw the distinct outline of fingers in the form of bruises on Julia's forearm.

"Julia...what happened?"

Realizing that pretending that nothing happened wasn't going to make the situation any better, nor would it stop Danny's questions, Julia gave in.

"Really...you don't need to be concerned," she unsuc-cessfully tried to deflect.

"David left last week to go back to New England. His fiancé begged for him to come home. You can't blame the man."

She continued, as tears formed in her eyes and slowly rolled down her cheeks.

"Well, Carl...there's just so much more work for him. He's stressed." She tried hard to convince Danny, and herself, that Carl's growing temper was a natural result of the extra burden he took on when his brother left. Danny shook his head slowly. He could feel an angry tide rising within.

The tears were steadily falling by now. She dabbed at her face with the apron, in an attempt to stem the salty droplets.

"Two days ago," she said between sobs, "he went on a bender...I...I didn't think anything of it...but the more he drank, the angrier he became...I tried to stay out of his way...tried to be no trouble."

Danny could take no more. He respected their marriage, but Carl had gone too far.

"Where is he?" Danny firmly asked.

"Danny...no...he's a good man...he's just stretched to the breaking point...it won't happen again," she pleaded.

"He's my husband...I...I love him," which sounded more like a question and less like a statement.

It was difficult for Danny to hear this, let alone hear Julia practically beg him to not harm Carl.

"I swear, Julia...I swear! If he hurts you again...." He couldn't finish his statement, worried that it would terrify Julia.

Julia stepped forward and kissed Danny on the cheek. He turned and walked out the back door. Danny wouldn't stay with the Banks that night; he couldn't stay. The night was spent eight miles away in the back of his wagon.

***

All the way back to the shop in Sacramento, Danny lamented about the situation Julia was in. He wanted to help, but he also wanted to respect boundaries. In his mind, Carl Banks destroyed any semblance of honor and integrity that he had in his marriage. It was a tough one to chew on, and it set heavily on his heart. He could only hope for the best for Julia, whatever that may be. The alternative would have him do bad things...very bad things.

He pulled into the yard at the shop with the empty wagon. Two of the men who worked for the company greeted Danny as he jumped down from the driver's seat. They led the team to the shop to unhitch the oxen and place them in the corral to be tended to. Danny had a sullen countenance that he tried to hide. He was mostly successful.

After brushing the dust from his clothes, Danny walked into the office and stowed his gear. Standing around the table was Jim, their employee Gonzales, and Pleasant Parker, one of the merchants who had a regular contract with the freighting company. They were all examining a map of the Southern Sierra Nevada Mountains, and more specifically, they were detailing the route that was being used from Visalia to the Kern River diggings. It appeared to Danny that Mr. Parker was considering the proposition of sending supplies south.

"From Stockton to Visalia the road is not bad...maybe three hundred miles or so," Gonzales said to the group of men as Danny moved in to join them.

"And this cutoff," Gonzales traced the line representing the route from Visalia to Linn's Valley, "it looks to be seventy or so miles."

"Whatcha think of that...what's it called? The Greenhorn Trail?" Kinney asked Gonzales.

"Looks to be a bear of a trail. Too steep for wagons," he looked to Kinney and Danny, "I wouldn't take a wagon up that."

"Hmm..." Kinney rubbed his chin, "What if we freighted Parker's goods in a wagon to Linn's Valley, and then from there we send everythin' up and over the trail by mule?"

Gonzales shrugged his shoulders and raised his eyebrows, "That should work...but it'll be tough going."

"How long do you all figure it'll take to get to the diggings?" Parker sought to cut to the chase.

Kinney tallied the miles and did a little figuring in his head.

"Maybe...if there are no problems or delays...twenty days or so. Something like that."

The group of men continued to discuss the details. They'd need a wagon and a team or two of oxen, six to eight mules, and four men to mind the teams and mules. Pulling out some paper, Jim calculated what it'd cost. It was a modest amount, but considering the profits to be made, Pleasant Parker believed the benefits outweighed the costs. He planned to send a representative to the region within the week to establish a store to sell his goods. A contract was drawn up, and all of the parties agreed to the terms and signed the document. In two weeks the goods would be accumulated, loaded onto the freight wagon, and sent south.

With the particulars out of the way and business concluded Parker left to begin his preparations. That left Danny, Jim, and Gonzales to talk about the logistics of freighting Parker's supplies to the Kern River. It was discussed that Gonzales was one of the men who they'd send south. Typically, he was the man who traveled from Sacramento to Stockton, and then on to Visalia. He'd made the run several times and was familiar with the road. They also decided to send two of their best mule packers, Ah Joe and a man who went by the name of Sam. These two employees, immigrants from China, were hard workers and enjoyed what they did. They wore American-style clothing, but chose to keep their queue—the front part of the head was shaved, the remaining hair grown long and kept in a single braid that ran down the back. All three of the men were more than capable, reliable, and professional. Danny volunteered to be the fourth man. He wanted to see the new country, but more than anything, he hoped it would divert his attention from thoughts of Julia.

Over the next two weeks, the routine runs were made to fulfill their contractual obligations. Supplies to distant sutlers and camps, machinery and lumber to mining operations converting to quartz, or hard-rock, mining, and an assortment of odds and ends that customers paid to have transported. Danny had another employee deliver the supplies on the American River route, under the excuse that he needed to prepare for the Kern River run. This was mostly true, but he was avoiding what could be an unpleasant situation with Julia and her husband.

The wagon to be used for the Kern River route was given a complete overhaul. Every moving part was examined to ensure that it was in good shape, questionable spokes were fixed, wheel lugs were tightened, and new grease was applied. Extra parts were also secured for the wagon. The mules, too, were given the once over. Their packing gear, especially the seams, were checked and reinforced. And each mule was given a new set of shoes, the often stubborn mules and farrier tolerating each other. All was ready by the departure date.

On a Monday morning, Jim, Danny, and Gonzales took the freight wagon and team of oxen over to Parker's store to load and secure his goods. Close to two thousand pounds sat in the bed of the wagon—dry goods, canned meats, clothing, boots, and tools. Essentially, anything that Parker could imagine would be in demand was loaded onto the wagon. By design, what he was having freighted to the diggings wasn't enough to supply every potential miner there, and the food staples weren't plentiful enough to last a group of miners for long. Parker hoped it would stimulate demand and lead to the establishment of a permanent outpost for his store; an extension of a trading empire that was his dream.

Goods secured, the team was taken back to the shop where tarps encased the wares, and additional items for the team, as well as personal items, were loaded onto the wagon and the mules. And with that, the men, team, and mules were ready for their run. If all went well, they would return within a month and a half and add the route to their area of routine service. Jim shook each man's hand, wished them luck and safety, and watched as they exited the yard and disappeared down the street.

***

A man alone with his thoughts will often conjure up happy memories of the past to while the time away. Or he may dwell on the negative, that which is causing him angst. It was the negative that Danny was trying to outrun by going on this run. Walking was almost therapeutic. The feel of the sun and the cool breeze heightened his senses, as did seeing the variety of trees and animals along the way. Added to that, his steps beat out a rhythmic cadence to little songs that he sang in his head. When he wasn't lost within himself, he talked with his compatriots. Well...he talked with them, but mostly it was with Gonzales. Ah Joe and Sam participated in some of the conversations, but they mostly talked with each other in Cantonese. Neither Danny nor Gonzales had the slightest idea what the two men were saying.

But his conversations with Gonzales were refreshing. Not only could he point out different sights along the road he was familiar with, but he had a different worldview than Danny. Antonio Marquez Gonzales, who preferred to be called Gonzales, was a native Californio. His parents came to California when it was ruled by Spain, his father working on one of the sprawling ranchos as a vaquero—a cowboy. The ranchos, often encompassing hundreds of square miles, were passed down from generation to generation, and the Indian laborers, vaqueros, and other workers had offspring who often remained on the rancho employed in the same jobs as their parents and grandparents. That was the situation with Gonzales. He was born on a rancho and became a vaquero like his father, his days spent in the saddle working for a family on land that wasn't his and never would be. Generations of rulers and ruled, living side by side on land that would soon fall under the jurisdiction of the United States.

Gonzales didn't harbor animosity toward the Americanos. They didn't take anything that he or his family personally owned. Sure, a large number of the ranchos were overrun by squatters, and family estates were confiscated if they couldn't produce a paper trail to validate their Spanish or Mexican Land Grant. But to Gonzales, the Americanos were mostly fair. Citizenship was offered to the former residents of Mexico, and several prominent Californios were elected to the State legislature and aided in the writing of the State Constitution. The dislike of foreign miners typically applied to those from China, Peru, Chile, and Mexico. American residents normally drew a line between Californios and foreigners, although that line did blur at times. On the whole, Gonzales, and a large number of other Californios, felt their future and fortunes were better off with the United States. They could point at the fact that in the six or so years since the Americanos arrived, sleepy hamlets were now growing towns, many industries were now present and growing, ports were burgeoning, and the population of California was now over

300,000. Granted, this was all made possible by the Gold Rush.

Truthfully, Gonzales was no different than men like Danny and Stephen, and the thousands of other emigrants to California. People like Gonzales now had more opportunities to live the life they chose. It was Gonzales' dream to save enough money to purchase land of his own, to have a family, and to pass on a legacy. When he was tied to a rancho, the chances of fulfilling that dream were extremely small. But now? He was only limited by his own effort. Judging from his work ethic, Danny believed that Gonzales would have that land and all that came with it, in no time at all.

The conversation and exchange of stories with Gonzales' helped to pass the long days. Danny told of his childhood of growing up in Missouri and working on his family's farm. He told Gonzales of his mother and father, and of his younger brother Seth, of going to school, and of his trek across the continent. Gonzales was just as enthralled with Danny's life as Danny was with his. They had lived different lives; different, but similar all the same. Dreamers and doers, now both occupied the same ground and were becoming the best versions of themselves each day. As they walked and talked they contemplated their other travel companions. Ah Joe and Sam were also chasing a dream, although Danny and Gonzales suspected that their childhoods were more comparable to each other than with those of the two Chinese men. Their curiosity remained unsatisfied since the language barrier kept most of Ah Joe and Sam's past a mystery. Maybe that was for the best, for it enabled Danny and Gonzales to create elaborate tales about the men that aided in their passing of time.

Compared to Danny's walk across the continent, traveling from Sacramento to Stockton, and then on to Visalia, was far from being a hardship. There were others on the road, but it wasn't a crowded race to a destination. The road itself to Visalia was an established track, with pockets of settlements gathered around the crossings of creeks and rivers. Between Sacramento and Stockton, men on foot, on horses and mules, and riding on buckboards and stages were a consistent sight. Like Sacramento, Stockton was also a growing town, serving as another jumping-off point to the Mother Lode, but also experiencing growth in the number of farmers and ranchers. But the crowds thinned out from Stockton to Visalia. There was an occasional team heading north, but the men from the J. Kinney Freighting Co. had the road mostly to themselves. Perhaps there were others in front of and behind them who kept the same pace; perhaps they were alone.

It took them seventeen days to reach Visalia from Stockton. Originally called Four Creeks, Visalia became the seat of Tulare County when that county was carved out of Mariposa County in 1852. Having marshy surrounds that watered an expanse of oak groves, the small population was slow in growth until gold was found on the Kern River. From that moment on, Visalia itself became a miniature outpost to the diggings, with the usual array of merchants, saloons, boarding houses, and services available to usher off the gold seeker and embrace them as they returned none-the-richer.

When Danny's crew reached Visalia, it still straddled the line between village and town. Resting for the afternoon, Gonzales led Danny to a merchant he'd delivered freight to over the past year and a half. This man, named Andrew Bradford, held the latest gossip and news. Most of what he heard was at least a week old, but it was as up-to-date as reasonably possible. They talked about how many people he figured had passed through Visalia headed to the diggings, including the fact that many residents had dropped what they were doing for that placer gold. Business for Bradford was consistent, especially in the sale of dry goods and fresh meat. According to Bradford, Parker's agent stayed the night in a boarding house in town and had continued to the Kern River a week before. As far as the conditions on the Greenhorn Trail, Bradford heard that a wagon could still travel with ease to Linn's Valley, but from there on, a wagon would be more trouble than it was worth. This was somewhat comforting to Danny. They'd planned to transfer all of the supplies to pack mules at Visalia. Knowing that wasn't necessary for about sixty-eight more miles meant they'd save time and wear and tear on the mules.

Hearing that it wasn't practical to use a wagon on the Trail also reassured Danny that their plan to use mules wasn't a waste and would play to their advantage. Danny and Gonzales thanked Bradford for the information, and they decided to camp overnight just outside of town.

With the morning came breakfast. The men had eaten trail food since Stockton, so consuming a home-cooked meal was a welcome experience. Danny and Gonzales feasted on eggs, steak, coffee, and biscuits at a local boarding house. Ah Joe and Sam cooked for themselves, preferring the cuisine of their homeland. Danny and his friend savored each bite and drink. They also relished the short amount of time spent talking with the proprietor's pretty daughters. It was the little pleasures that often made life even sweeter than it was. Full of food, the two men headed back to the team, prepared for the next leg of the run. With a bellyful of food, they were uncomfortable for the rest of the morning, but with no regrets, they believed it was well worth every morsel of food they consumed. Life is also full of small sacrifices.

Four more days of travel placed the group in Linn's Valley. They were now on the outer edge of the Greenhorn Trail. Just like almost every other place they'd been in California, this valley was a beautiful sight to behold. With small creeks flowing down from the mountains, lush grass that swept across draws and flats, and broad oak trees forming a canopy that provided shade, God's hand touched the land. There were just a few settlers here, their homes clustered a short distance from each other. He imagined he, too, could make a life there as a farmer or a rancher. Maybe even open a little restaurant or business with a wife. Maybe someone like Julia. To his credit, he hadn't thought much of Julia, but it was difficult to not think of her when he encountered such beauty and thoughts of his life in the future. He needed to try harder to tamp down thoughts of her or risk losing his focus on life. Luckily, there was work to be done.

Unsure how much farther it was until the Greenhorn Trail turned too rugged to haul freight with the buckboard, Danny and Gonzales decided to scout ahead, a good practice when traversing unfamiliar land. They left Ah Joe and Sam in Linn's Valley with the team and mules and began walking south along the eastern edge of Linn's Valley, crossing shallow draws and washes as they went. Walking for a few hours, they were relatively sure that the oxen-drawn buckboard could move several miles along, perhaps as far as Poso Flat. By the time they returned to the team, it was late in the afternoon, but instead of staying over in Linn's Valley, they made as many miles as they could until evening, choosing a pleasant campsite near a cluster of large granite boulders and giant white oak trees. The night was cool and clear, and with the moon just a sliver in the sky, the stars were magnificent. A million sparkles in the sky, twinkling, almost blinking. As Danny was fading off to sleep, the campfire just a bed of coals, he saw a shooting star. He felt blessed and internally at ease with himself and the world around him.

***

The next morning led to much of the same thing that had happened over the last month. They ate, they packed, and they hit the Trail. Within three hours they finally reached Poso Flat. Unlike Linn's Valley, the valley containing Poso Flat was much narrower. The Poso Creek ran down from the mountains, and with enough rain or melting snow, it could be a formidable obstacle to cross, but it was May of 1854, and the water was not so deep that they couldn't walk across the slowly moving water. It was in this valley that the Greenhorn Trail began its climb east up a ridge of the Greenhorn Mountains. And it was here that the men would have to unload the goods from the wagon and repack all of it on mules. This took some skill, and attention had to be paid when balancing loads. Too much weight and the mule would rebel. A lopsided load interfered with the mules' balance, and the mule would rebel. Come to think of it, a mule can be a cantankerous creature, not needing much provocation to rebel. That's why the men carefully prepared their loads and were experienced in handling the beasts. This would, hopefully, allow them to avoid any pitfalls a tenderfoot packer may experience.

With the mules loaded and as ready as they'd ever be, Danny, Ah Joe, and Sam left Gonzales with the buckboard. Looking at the rough map of the Trail they had with them, they figured that the agent at the diggings was within fifteen or so miles. Not knowing exactly where he was, they took four days' worth of rations with them. Surely, when they ran across a group of miners they could point the group in the right direction.

Onward they trudged, at first up a gentle incline that began up the ridge. Danny was in front of the mule train, leading the group through little pockets of oak trees. The going wasn't as brisk as traveling on the road, but they were making progress. Soon, however, that retched Trail gained in elevation. The Greenhorn Trail, with its loose rocks and ruts cut deep through the trail, slowed down the momentum of man and beast. Despite the fact they were trudging up the ridge in the coolness of the late morning, the shade provided by the stands of oak became less consistent. They found themselves walking a path cut through chaparral, sage, scrub oak, and a lone oak tree here and there. The sun beat down on them, and despite the cool air, they were soon sweating and looking ahead on the trail for the next patch of shade and respite from the sun. Danny was not certain, but he guessed that the intensified discussion between Ah Joe and Sam was full of curse words and damnation. This wasn't the easy walking they'd grown used to over the last month, and their thighs burned to remind them.

Poso Flat sits at an elevation of just over 2,400 feet above sea level. At the top of the Greenhorn Trail, before it begins to drop down to the diggings, the elevation was a tad over 5,000 feet. The gain in elevation the pack train was making felt like progress until the Trail dipped through a saddle; going down a ridge only to continue the climb one hundred yards on made it feel like they were erasing any gain they'd made. Danny imagined that if they'd tried to drag and push the buckboard up the Trail it'd be a hellish experience; not impossible, but not simply done. As it was, the mules periodically lost their footing on the loose granite and soil, momentarily stumbling, but recovering quickly.

With a mile of the Trail underfoot, Danny found a nice spot in the shade to rest the train, the small grove of skinny black oak dropped the temperature of the surrounding area, or at least the area touched by the shade. The slight breeze, coupled with the sheen of sweat each man wore, cooled their skin. After taking a hearty drink from their canteens, the men adjusted the loads on the mules, repositioning and tightening the straps and harnesses. Hoping to make the top of the Trail by mid-afternoon, they continued their march.

Danny was uncertain how much farther they had to go. The map he had wasn't much help, it just illustrated a jagged line running from Poso Flat up into the Greenhorn Mountains, and down to the Kern River. There was no scale or legend, just a line drawn as if to say "struggle this way to the diggings!" Looking up the trail did nothing for the men, either. They might see one or two hundred yards ahead, but the trail turned, or dropped, or crested another hilltop. Looking to the south was no help, for more ridges ran parallel east and west. The only indication of where the Trail might meet the pass was by looking to the north. Across the valley that contained Poso Flat was a pine and oak-studded mountain, with a ridge that ran the same direction as the one they were on. Now and then, Danny caught a glimpse of the narrowing valley to the east. It appeared that the mountain ridge to the north and the ridge they were presently on eventually met, creating a choke point. Danny surmised that the Greenhorn Trail must plateau around that point, but it was just a guess.

Mouths dry and muscles aching, they reached a small meadow with tall, green grass. It was flat ground, but more importantly, again, there was shade. Danny and his men drank more water and ate some jerky while the mules browsed a bit. Looking around, Danny mentally compared his current surroundings with that of the American

River. For the most part, it was a night and day difference. The land here was dry, the vegetation densely clustered on the side of the mountain. The valleys and meadows were similar, but it looked much drier. And the creeks here were small and shallow. Maybe the Kern River would be more like the American River. Soon enough he'd find out. But he and the pack train had to make it over this path.

They continued up the Trail another mile and a half. All was still progressing well, but the mules were acting skittish. The men checked the loads to ensure they hadn't been displaced, but nothing was amiss. Danny couldn't figure out what was troubling them. He did spot some bear scat along a portion of the trail, probably belonging to a black bear, but there was always a chance it could be a grizzly. That could've spooked the animals. It could also be any number of things—coyotes, wolves, mountain lions. It was hard to say. Besides being stubborn creatures, mules put up a Hell of a fight when they needed to, kicking and stomping their attacker. They'd even been known to bite and toss animals threatening them. Maybe they were on alert because of a threat. Maybe they were just being mules. Either way, the men worked to calm them and maintain control of the pack train.

Perhaps another mile or so was passed underfoot when they reached a small knoll with a large white oak tree off to the side and a cluster of flat boulders near another set of smaller black oaks. Like a common theme, it was another resting point largely dictated by its relative flatness and ample shade. From the looks of the hills, it seemed that the Trail was now leveling out, for the most part. It was still gaining in elevation, but the angles were different, closer to horizontal than vertical. Danny thought that they may be nearing the top of the trail, but he couldn't tell for sure.

It was now nearing early afternoon and the team needed some rest. They hitched the pack train to the big oak tree, the lead long enough for the mules to chew on grass and brush, but not so long that they could wander off or get tangled up in anything. Ah Joe and Sam sat down on the flat boulders and marveled at the grooves worn into the granite. Curious if the path would become easier, or even if they were close to the top, Danny told the men that he was going to scout out the path. He grabbed his shotgun from the pack of one of the mules, checked to make sure it was loaded, grabbed his canteen, and headed up the path.

Walking without the mules was much quicker, and Danny covered another mile with ease. He passed several more small meadows and spotted in the distance what he believed to be seeps where water bubbled to the surface. More than likely, if he dug in those seeps a small spring would form. It'd be a nice home site if someone chose to plant some roots there.

Venturing on, what he figured to be another half a mile, the Trail ran down the side of the ridge and onto a flat. And just a quarter of a mile down that flat was the best natural spring he'd seen on that mountain. It'd also be an ideal spot for a home site, or, at the very least, another place to rest the mules. They might even make camp for the night right there.

The pass looked to be another mile or so to the east, for the ridges to the north and south came together in the distance. Danny had been gone for a little over an hour. If he hurried back, and if the mules cooperated, they could make it to the good spring before dark, unload the mules, make dinner, and relax for the evening. It was a realistic goal.

Danny retraced his steps, finding it much more pleasant to walk down the Trail. It was still warm, but he wasn't sweating as much as before. Surely, that'd change when they headed back up the path to the spring in the distance. Until then, he'd just enjoy the walk. The angle of the sun, lower in the sky than it was a few hours ago, altered the shadows and gave Danny a different perspective than when he'd walked in the other direction. His father always said that each step had a thousand different views. From Danny's experience, his father was correct. Someday, he thought, he wanted to bring his mother, father, and brother out to California. They'd tour every place Danny had worked and visited, and they'd go to see the Pacific Ocean. Maybe even put their feet in that big body of water. If business continued the way it was, Danny would have a modest fortune, and that wasn't even figuring in the take from Julia's Kitchen. He couldn't envision himself going back home now. There were too many opportunities in the new State. Perhaps his family would be willing to leave Missouri permanently for California.

He was getting closer to where he'd left the men and the pack train. A half a mile, and then a quarter of a mile. As with the hike up the Greenhorn Trail, he couldn't see much distance down the path, but he knew he was getting near. Once he was one hundred yards away from the resting spot he heard the mules. They were fussing about and braying, clearly unhappy with something. Danny figured they'd caught wind of other animals, or maybe they heard or smelled him. The more time he spent with those animals, the less he seemed to understand them.

As he dropped down the little ridge he could still hear the mules, but they were shielded from sight by the trees and brush. It could be that Sam and Ah Joe were refitting the mules. Fifty yards out, Danny decided to razz them a bit.

"Ah Joe...Sam! Is that you making all that noise? What're you boys doing?" Danny hollered to them as he came down the trail.

"Hey...there's a spring a ways up the path. Might be a nice place...What the Hell?" he stopped midsentence and tried to comprehend what he saw.

Hung from the big white oak was a man. He only saw the backside of the man, but it appeared to be Sam. His braid was cut, and his neck was grotesquely stretched. Sam, hung lifeless, his bodily fluids released; a last insult to his condition.

Hoping there was still a chance to save Sam, Danny ran toward the big oak tree, yelling, "Sam! Oh my God...Sam!"

Quickly approaching the tree, he tossed his shotgun. He was focused on Sam, losing his wits and ignoring the how and why the body was in the tree in the first place. Right before he reached Sam, a man stepped from behind the tree and swung a pickaxe handle at Danny's head. Caught by surprise, and with too much momentum, the handle collided with Danny's head with an audible thump. Danny's head snapped backwards, opposite of his momentum, his feet flew out from beneath him, and his body crashed down to the hard ground. Barely conscious, he felt the flow of blood from his head. It ran down into his left ear and left eye, clouding his already blurring vision.

"Remember me, you sum-bitch?" George, one of the Roberts Boys yelled at the prone Danny who was struggling to breathe and remain conscious.

Rolling slowly to his side and then his stomach, Danny attempted to get up, only making it to one knee before George hit him with the handle again, this time on the right side of his ribcage. The air sucked out of his lungs, Danny fell back down and rolled to his side in agony. Tears mixed with blood in a liquid mess.

Fighting back the blackness, Danny heard men laughing. There was more than just one man. Through his cloudy haze, he saw two men rifling through the goods packed on the mules.

"This hear is all good stuff," a man who he believed to be Harry said to the other two men.

"No sense in letting it go to waste...they're not gonna use it," said Eli, and the men roared with laughter.

Danny groaned and turned his head upward. Above him was Sam, his face twisted and blueish-grey. The breeze slowly turned his body in a slow semi-circle. Danny coughed, his lips coated with his blood causing a red mist to fly from his mouth.

"Whatcha wanna do with this boy," George asked as he kicked Danny in the stomach. Danny doubled over even more, curled into a fetal position.

"String 'em up with his Chinee friend," Eli flatly said. "They deserve each other."

Danny was in the fight of his life without throwing a single punch. He wasn't fighting these Roberts Boys. He was fighting death itself. The pain was excruciating, and he fought back the feeling of darkness. At the mercy of the Roberts Boys, there wasn't much Danny was able to do other than just try to keep his body alive...and he felt as though he was losing.

George set the pick handle against the big oak, walked to a horse that was tied to a bush, and returned with a short piece of rope. Kneeling, he roughly rolled Danny onto his stomach, grabbed his right and left hands, and bound them together behind his back. Danny managed a weak, "no...please," to nobody who cared.

"Bring that mule over here," George called to Harry. It was the mule, cleared of its gear, which they'd used as a platform to string up Sam.

"Give me a hand, here! Hell...he already feels like dead weight," George said to Harry as he struggled to pick Danny up.

"You made a funny, George," Eli said with a chuckle. "He'll be dead soon enough."

Eli walked over to Danny and looked over his blood-covered face.

"Problem with you, farmer boy, is you never know when to quit...never know when to give in to your betters."

He lifted Danny's chin to get a better look, and with a disgusted tone stated, "Damn...you're a mess. Better make peace with your maker."

They lifted Danny's limp body onto the back of the mule, and he slumped forward, laying against the mule's neck. Eli quickly tied a noose out of rope from Parker's supplies, like he'd done it more than one other time, and then threw the weighted end over a branch in the large white oak tree. Giving it slack, and then pulling it up, he positioned it at the correct height and tied it off to the tree. The noose hung low enough for it to be slipped over

Danny's head and tightened around his neck, but high enough to ensure that his body would dangle above the ground.

As his body lay against the mule he prayed. Not for himself, but for Sam, and his family, and for Julia. He and God were good. Although he didn't go to church on any type of regular basis, he believed in God. Silently, he prayed every night, thanking God for his life and his protection. And as he walked from Sacramento to this very spot, the spot that would see the end of his life, he looked about and saw God's touch. God was everywhere.

They sat Danny up and lifted his, slipped the noose around his head, and cinched it tight around his neck. Just sitting there was putting upward pressure on his neck, making it difficult to breathe. Danny mouthed the word "no" while looking at the three men. His feeble plea was ignored.

"Wonder if he'll piss himself like the heathen?" George wondered out loud.

"Jesus, George," Harry answered, of course he will."

Eli slapped the mule on the rump, causing the animal to jump at the shock and then run forward.

Danny's body slipped off the mule and was caught by the rope, suspending him in the air. He struggled against gravity, his legs kicking as he struggled for footing that wasn't there. Danny was being strangled, the darkness he'd fought minutes before creeping forward, enveloping his thoughts and his sight. As his kicking body spun and swung, Danny could see the men watching, pleased with their work. Suffocating, Danny slipped toward unconsciousness, darkness turning from a terrifying thought to a comforting reality. Death was here.

In his final moment of lucidity, his neck stretched and burning, Danny heard a sickening crack. It was a splintering crack as the branch used to suspend him above the ground gave way to his weight and broke away from the ancient white oak tree. In the fight with death, gravity won. Danny's body landed feet first and crumpled to the ground, followed soon after by the branch that crashed to the earth across his legs.

Astonished, the Roberts Boys rushed over to Danny's limp body.

"Never seen that before! Should we string him up again?" George asked Eli.

"Naw...we got better things to do. No use in hangin' a dead man twice! Let the buzzards pick his bones."

The Roberts Boys gathered their horses, each man taking a string of mules. They rode up the Greenhorn Trail without speaking, disappearing from the area within minutes.

***

Daniel Vance, on the cusp of twenty-four years of age, lay without motion on the ground. His skin was pale, his hair matted with blood, and his face looked to be partially painted a maroon color.

His body lay in state for several hours, undisturbed. Danny wondered if this was what it was like to be dead. A big nothingness? Blackness and searing pain? A faint awareness of a vibrating body and whispering voices?

Whispering voices? What are they saying? He tried to concentrate through the pain. Angels? Were they angels? Or maybe his ancestors, beckoning him to a proverbial light?

The darkness, intense and consuming at first, began to fade. And as it did, he became more aware of pain—pain in his ribs; pain in his head; and pain in his legs. He also felt his body rocking. Were they spasms or convulsions? Was he having a seizure?

Rocking; body rocking. Rocking and pain. The man was rubbing Danny's sternum, trying to stimulate his blood flow and bring him back to consciousness.

"Boy...you alive boy?" Danny faintly heard a voice saying.

"Come on, son...come on around," the stranger said to the prone Danny. He'd already removed the noose and lifted the branch from his legs.

Danny swam through the shrinking darkness in his mind. With great difficulty he managed to open his right eye; his left eye was sealed shut with dried blood. Unfocused, he looked toward the sky only to see the outline of a face. In his semi-conscious state, he became acutely aware of his pain, as well as his parched lips and dry mouth.

The man placed a hand under the back of Danny's head and gently lifted it.

"Here...take a sip of this water," as the man tipped a canteen to Danny's lips to let a trickle of the cool substance fall into his mouth. "Just a sip."

Danny quickly drank down the water and choked, sputtering and coughing.

"Careful, now boy...careful."

Taking more care, Danny once again sipped and swallowed a small amount of water. His vision, still mostly blurred, momentarily returned allowing him to stare into the face of an older, bearded man with a worn slouch hat decorated with a hawk's feather. It was a friendly face, especially compared to the faces of the Roberts Boys.

Danny opened his mouth to say something, but pain once again shot through his body, reverberating from his head to his throat, to his side. An intense pain, it was overwhelming. Danny slipped back into darkness, the man's face fading from his consciousness. Death didn't claim another soul on that day. Death would have to wait.

***

To be continued...

Book 2: Preview

————•••◆•••————

The Following Is A Preview of Book 2 in the
Golden Empire Series:

A Good Stock

Available Now!

A Brewing Storm

———•◦◆◦•———

Juglans Nigra, otherwise known as the Eastern Black Walnut, grows wild along riparian zones in eastern North America. Often reaching heights over one hundred feet tall with an elongated, straight trunk when allowed room to grow, this versatile tree can be found as far north as Ontario, Canada, west to South Dakota, all the way down to Florida, and to the southwest into Texas. It's a species that provides much to many—the soil, animals, and humans.

A hearty tree, its roots take to the earth quickly and stake a claim on life, allowing for an increased survival rate of seedlings and the extension of their lifespan for as long as one hundred and thirty years.

Within four to six years this variety of tree is mature enough to produce fruit that ripens in autumn; a tasty nut, encased in a hard shell, shrouded by a brownish-green soft husk. A walnut—the seed that is eaten when broken free of its casing; the same seed that begins the life cycle of new trees.

The Eastern Black Walnut, like other lifeforms, competes for survival. Precious resources, such as minerals, water, and sunlight are sought out as necessities. For many species of flora and fauna, survival is a matter of luck and timing. Did a seed sprout amidst a congested forest? Was there a drought? Did wildlife happen to choose the growing, young stem or roots as a meal? Were insects sweeping through the region? Did all of the perfect conditions exist at exactly the right time for the sapling to mature into a mighty walnut tree? Most plant life has no control over the situation.

There are some species, however, that have the ability to gain an advantage over the competition. The walnut tree is one of these. It is allelopathic, with the ability to release chemicals from its roots that harm and inhibit the growth of other plant forms to give it an edge in the game of survival. An adaptive tactic, it isn't unlike what humans are capable of to give themselves an advantage over others. People like the Roberts Boys, who steal, rob, intimidate, and kill to get what they want. Caustic parasites, the Roberts Boys don't give their unfortunate victims a chance, for they prey on the weak and unsuspecting, and a fair fight isn't in their vocabulary. Victims, like Danny Vance and his friend, Sam, are subject to the nonexistent mercy of the Roberts Boys.

Outwardly, a walnut tree is attractive, the grayish-black bark arranged in a diamond pattern from the trunk to its heavy branches; individual diamonds like scale armor, separate entities united as one living organism. To the trained and untrained noses alike, these trees emanate a spicy or bitter odor, not entirely unpleasant nor appealing, but distinct all the same. That fragrant, decorated bark covers and protects a straight-grained wood that is deep brown in color, and desired for its durability and strength, yet ease to work. In the hands of a skilled craftsman, the wood from a walnut tree can be transformed into beautiful cabinets, tables, and other useful and attractive types of furniture that display the pattern of the grain. Used in flooring, the maintained planks are capable of outlasting the people who laid it down and walked upon it daily.

This type of wood is also desirable in the construction of coffins, the final home of the human shell that embodied the newly departed spirit. A number of the victims of the Roberts Boys weren't given the pleasure of being lowered into the ground in a fancy coffin. Their soulless bodies withered away off well-traveled paths, victims first of the brutality of the Roberts Boys, and second of the elements.

In the hands of a skilled craftsman, a block of walnut can be turned into a work of art. Cut to the correct length and width, a craftsman begins to shave and shape the wood, eventually to the point where a smoothing plane is used to create a piece of wood free of burrs and pits. It is now a piece of polished wood with a purpose; with angles and curves, maybe even a grove, designed to provide support and absorb shock.

Affixed to this handsome piece of wood is a tube of iron that was first heated and rolled around a chemise in one-foot sections, welded into three-foot lengths, reheated and worked, and then eventually hollowed out to a uniform circumference with a boring bit. It was now a part of a tool, an instrument capable of bringing death and destruction in the hands of skilled and unskilled alike. One shot at a time. The shotgun is a dependable and devastating weapon at close to medium range. A man doesn't have to be a marksman to carry out his intentions with this weapon. Aimed in a general direction, and with the squeeze of a trigger, a controlled explosion propels multiple amounts of lead down the barrel out toward the intended target. The impact of the shot is largely dependent on the distance and size of the lead pellets, but it ranges from the creation of a hole large enough to fit a man's fist into, to a wide pattern of entrance wounds sprinkled across a surface.

A shotgun, like any firearm, is an inanimate tool. By itself, it was just wood and iron, absent of motive and action. However, in the hands of a man intent on destruction, it is a tool very capable of the job. Like a hammer designed to drive a nail, a shotgun's purpose is clear and effective. But they both require human hands to carry out their designed purpose.

At that moment, this product of skilled craftsman-ship—shaped wood from a walnut tree and rolled, welded, and bored iron tubing—was being wiped down and oiled. As the man removed the dirt and bits of debris, as well as the beginnings of rust on the barrel, he admired the sleek curves and coolness of the metal. The grain of the wood was especially attractive. It was one of the things he and his brother fawned over the most when they originally received the firearm as a gift from their grandfather. He appreciated the time and effort that was taken in its cre-ation, the skill of the craftsman evident in every part of the weapon. Creation was not what this man intended. Justice was what he was after. Violence was largely his intent. The hands caressing and cleaning this implement of wood and iron belonged to Danny Vance, and vengeance weighed heavily on his mind.

Note To Readers

———•••◆•••———

Researching and writing is something I do for fun. This isn't my career. I enjoy the challenge. In a sense, it is personally and professionally satisfying to me. As I like to joke, it's my side hustle. I also enjoy talking with people who have read my books and hearing praise and ideas on how my writing and storylines could be improved. That's all part of the process for me. Sadly, though, my readers typically don't leave many reviews of my books on marketplaces like Amazon. Because of a very competitive market, many readers won't give my books a chance because they depend on the reviews of others to guide their choices. And the lack of reviews means that my books get less notice because of the algorithms on Amazon.

So, even if you don't have the time or desire to write a complete review (which is understandable), if you can please at least give it a rating that would be both pleasing to me and helpful. My sincere thanks!

About The Author

---◆---

R ichard Roux was born in Bakersfield, California, and has resided there his whole life. By profession, he is a social studies teacher at Centennial High School and an adjunct history professor at Bakersfield Community College. With an interest in a wide variety of topics and activities, Richard brings to his writing a mixture of history, anecdotes, and humor. When not spending time with his family, teaching, playing hockey, and enjoying the outdoors, he continues to research and write a mixture of nonfiction and fiction works.